The Last Resort

– A Story of No Intrinsic Worth –

Josh Caverton

Copyright©2018JoshCaverton

All rights reserved.

ISBN:9781726399319
ISBN-1726399311

DEDICATION

To the irrational, the meaningless, and the frightening.
To not thinking it through, and to the total opposite.

"Wendy? Darling? Light of my life. I'm not gonna hurt ya. You didn't let me finish my sentence. I said, I'm not gonna hurt ya. I'm just going to bash your brains in."

- Jack Torrance, *The Shining*

"We're gonna make some big decisions in our little world."

- Bob Ross, *The Joy of Painting*

INT. EXECUTIVE OFFICE – DAY

The movie executive conducts his hands into a triangle of thought and power, leans back in his leather swivel chair (imported from Portugal) and prepares to listen. He is wearing a plain charcoal suit with no tie, the top two buttons of his shirt undone. There is nothing on the desk in front of him—no computer or desk pad. The space is clean and ready for ideas.

The filmmaker is wearing a khaki photographer's vest with lots of pockets. This lends him the air of someone who likes to get things done, although it also makes him look like he's on safari. He shuffles and clears his throat: "The film opens with someone's face—a guy, in his twenties, relatively good looking, but not jocular or threatening. There's a touch of nerd in the face, but *only* a touch. He's your average graphic novel reader, the kind of guy who likes to think he's highbrow—maybe he can remember a poem or two from school, reads a couple of books a year. That's our guy. The camera's square on his face and he's looking quizzical."

"I'm with you," the exec says, his finger triangle opening at its top for a moment as he points at the filmmaker with both index fingers. "But what's behind this guy? I mean physically—I'm just thinking *mise en scène*. Are we inside, are we outside, what?"

"Great question," says the filmmaker. "Glad you asked. We're talking natural light, although with the even neutrality of shade—no chiaroscuro, no hints of noir. At the very edges of the frame, the tiny slices where we might get backdrop, think blue sky. There needs to be the sense this guy is outdoors. For the viewer, though, the sense is going to be an instinctual one. It won't be something they'll cognitively register, and that's because of the voiceover fading in gradually and pulling us out of silence. You're going to be hearing a woman's voice—perky, working class British, so missing a lot of the Gs and Hs. She sounds late teens or mid-twenties, and she's talking about how her life is going great and how she wants to thank not only all her friends but the whole world for the opportunities she's been given and boy is she lucky to be living such a blessed life etcetera etcetera. And this is going to be backed with fairly light, fairly uplifting instrumental. I tend to describe audio best through an appeal to visuals: think of the music as the audio equivalent of spring mornings, silhouettes of toned women in yoga poses next to sea views, then mix that with some teddy bears sharing honey and holding heart-shaped balloons."

"Hmm," says the exec sceptically.

"Bear with me," says the filmmaker. "The juxtaposition here is vital. Remember, we're still looking at our protagonist's face, our mid-twenties pseudo-nerd film-watching everyman. He's still the dominant aspect of the frame, and what we're seeing is roughly the same expression you just gave me—if you excuse my invasion of your face. He's moving from quizzical to the vague fringes of repelled, the delicate dint of disgust. But as this is happening, we're also slowly zooming in, slowly venturing closer to his left eye, until we can see the reverse image of what he sees—because we're *really* zooming in here. We're getting ultra-close, right into the pupil itself, and then we're living in the slightly convex reflection, and what we see is this guy's phone (that's what he's looking at), the lit-up digital screen—reversed, of course—and it's floating in black (and this can be done digitally—I've already created a mock of how it'll look) and the phone screen flips over so we can read it, so it's no longer a mirror image, and all the while we're still moving in this impossible zoom toward the screen, until, eventually, it resolves itself on this girl's Facebook post. The voiceover suddenly matches up with the words on the screen, so now the girl is clearly reading her bubbly post to us and everything starts to make sense."

"So our protagonist is reading a Facebook post by some optimistic moron?"

"Exactly!"

"Then what happens?"

"Well, here's the innovative part. As we reach the bottom of the woman's post and it finishes with something awful like 'hashtag living life' or some shit like that, the screen scrolls up in a way that very clearly indicates our protagonist is using his finger to control the movement—everyone understands that movement these days, it's basically hardwired into contemporary visual literacy—and we land on the picture that's attached to the post. It's the girl, and she's on a beach in this perfectly saturated image: amazing explosive colour, the sea is popping in the background, there's a thin line of tropical mountainside in the corner, and in the foreground she's sitting cross-legged and she's in her bikini—"

"She's hot, right?"

"Oh, yeah, of course. But in the characteristic way you see in these kinds of photos. Nice body, tanned, and she's smiling and looking off to her left at some life-affirming joke the viewer can't see, the sun bouncing off sunglasses that are very definitely this season. It's all there. It's an immediate envy photo—a status anxiety bomb designed to explode in the viewers' lives. Like, why is this girl living this life and why am I stuck in mine, why am I fat and ugly and masturbatory. Why am I poor? The photo is utilising all the tropes and tics of Generation Selfie, and it should make the critical viewer either crushingly depressed or hurl them into a homicidal rage."

"And it'll make them horny, right?"

"Absolutely. Without a doubt."

"Good. I think that's important."

The filmmaker smiles and continues with the same enthusiasm. "At this point, while we're focusing on the image of this woman, the fluffy music fades out as the scratchy sound of wind fades in, and simultaneously we see the filters drop away from the image: the gentle lens flare in the corner goes, the warm sepia additions are subtracted, the slightly adjusted contrast is eliminated, and the picture begins to feel very flat and very real. Yes, it's still a tropical beach somewhere, but it now has the visual blandness of reality—that glary overexposure that makes you squint and feel tired. And then the image begins moving, the sea takes on the ripple of real time, and in the background—rather close—we see the bottom half of a fat guy move by, hairy gut hanging down and garish Batman board shorts. Our girl still isn't moving though. It's clear she's really holding this pose—that the insouciance is insincere. Then she speaks, just moving her mouth, not turning to the camera, and she says, "Ave ya taken it yet?' And her voice is pretty far from the bubbly optimistic one we heard in the initial voiceover. I mean, it's the same voice, but without the composure. It's aggressive and ticked off. You can immediately hear the horror of self-indulgence and some of the evil inherent in her narcissism. Then the male voice from behind the camera says, 'Yeah, but lemme get a couple more so ya got somefing to choose from.' At this point we incorporate a slight wobble in the frame to reinforce the hand-held point-of-view of the photographer, and simultaneously we see the woman sigh and shuffle, and then she says, in that same awful tone, 'Well stop being such a faggit about it and take em.' The filmmaker pauses for a moment and eases back into his seat, trying to gauge how the exec has taken this word, whether he's appreciating the rapid characterisation.

"So this woman's a bitch," he says, understanding his cue and once again opening his triangle to point his index fingers.

"Exactly!" says the filmmaker.

"And are we going to find out more about her? Is she going to get naked? And I assume she's linked in some way to our original character—the face. An ex-girlfriend?"

"Yes, we will find out more; yes, she is certainly going to get naked—the market demands it. And yes, she will be connected to the main character, although exactly how she's connected is an important reveal later on."

"Good, okay."

The filmmaker leans forward again. "Okay, so we've just heard her call this offscreen guy a faggot. At this point, we get our first real cut of the film. Everything up until now has been one unbroken flow of images. Now the cut happens and we've got a loose close-up of a guy wearing some aviator sunglasses. Behind him you can see a bustling tourist resort with blurry South-East Asian bits and pieces—pagodas, palm trees, stuff like that. Even without the aid of any cutaways the viewer gets the sensation of Thailand, a holiday resort for Westerners, that sort of thing. All this augments the first visual impression of this guy as a sort of British lout. We've already heard his voice and it's got more than a hint of chav about it. And now we can see his footballer haircut *du jour* and thick bulldog neck and stoic mouth. This is a guy who goes to the gym and cares about his body, and even without any more info you could safely bet that he's got some unfashionable tribal tattoo on one of his oversized arms. He's a run-of-the-mill fuckboy. But here's the big reveal: he takes off his aviators—which really make him look like a porno thug—and we see his eyes. Casting is vital here. His eyes are genuinely sad—they're these melancholy eyes, puppy-esque, but also just quite dumb. When the viewer looks into them, they *get* this guy, they get everything about him: not great in school but fundamentally decent. Slow but lovely. A sad victim of the sharp and shallow aspects of life—and also someone who's going to be easy to lead around. He's a modern Lenny."

"Lenny?"

"*Of Mice and Men*. Retard who breaks a woman's neck...? Steinbeck." The exec nods, although the filmmaker is not entirely certain the reference has been effective. He forges on. "Anyway, our guy's not quite that level—he's not actually special needs. Just nice and dumb. So the audience sees this, and they can see that he's sad— that being called a faggot has hurt him. And he breathes out, breathes in, then says in a pretty sheepish voice, 'Soph, I jus wanna make ya look pretty.' We cut back to a shot of Sophie, and it's clear she's immune to the cuteness of this guy's lumbering and easily damaged innocence, and she barks at him: 'Fuck, Olly, jus take the fucken photo! Christ.' Then she's back to smiling her smile at the imaginary offscreen amusement, her face a total rictus. We cut back to Olly, who puts his sunglasses back on, holds up his phone again to take another photo—sticking his tongue out a little in a way that suggests concentration (which will add to the establishment of a childlike persona) then we cut on the sound of the camera clicking and boom, we find ourselves transported to their hotel room for a brief sex scene."

"I like it—getting straight in there."

"It's what the audience wants—you give them nudity in the first five minutes and then they feel anything is possible."

"And they're turned on."

"Sure."

"What are you thinking regarding the sex?"

"Well, it needs to be quick—no more than three or four seconds. It has to be loud, almost theatrical, because here again juxtaposition is king, and I want it to characterise Sophie as someone who acts as if some invisible audience is watching her all the time. I'd quite like to mimic the scene from *Trainspotting*—he's on his back, she's on top, the viewers watching the wild writhing from a side-on long-shot. And I want the moment to finish with Sophie slapping him hard in the face while she rides him—the *slap* is the cut, a nice hard edge on which to change scene, and suddenly we're at a beach bar in a two-shot, Olly on the left, Sophie on the right, the ocean behind them. She's on her phone and he's just staring into the middle distance and neither one of them is saying anything."

"I like it a lot." The exec leans back. "So let's lay this out: we've got a guy checking his phone, and on the phone he sees Sophie's inane post about how great her life is, then we zoom in to Sophie's holiday, discover she's actually awful, then meet her idiot boyfriend. We watch them have sex, then *el smacko,* we settle into their ennui." The exec puts his hands on the table and measures his thoughts before speaking. "There are a lot of positive elements to this project so far. What happens next?"

EXT. BEACH BAR – DAY

Olly's mind itched and flickered. He was thinking of muzzles, then he was staring at the coloured labels on the liquor bottles, then he was thinking of muzzles again. He was finding it difficult to focus, and despite the evidently good things that were happening to him—he was on holiday, he'd just had sex—he didn't feel happy. Next to him Sophie was locked to her phone with a look of intense concentration. He knew well enough not to bother her.

He turned and gazed at the ocean: digital blue, wide and placid. He took a deep breath of humid air and decided it tasted faintly of spice. They'd saved hard for this trip and he wanted to enjoy it. Seven days to soak up as much sun and sea and erotica as possible before East London recalled them and he found himself back on a building site under a grey sky. They'd already used most of day one, and he tried to convince himself that it had been a good time by examining the objective facts: he had spent it on a beach, drinking beer, his toes in the sand. He'd dipped in and out of seawater that had no right to be as warm and clear as it was. And he'd had sex. These were good things.

Yet something wasn't sitting right.

The journey itself had been an ordeal. The couple had argued badly during the boarding process at Heathrow, and the resulting silent treatment naturally led Olly to believe it was *his* fault that Sophie had misunderstood the government restrictions on carrying fluids. He'd had time to think about what he'd done during the twelve-hour flight. With his six-foot-three frame he sat in the middle seat, rigid and awake while his girlfriend (on his left) and a man he didn't know (on his right) slumbered against his shoulders. By the time they'd landed and switched to the resort-bound coach, his eyes were red and filmy, his body sore.

Their room, however, was exactly what had been promised in the ads, first floor and with beach access, and once they were in Sophie was extremely excited. Arrival had been like a line of cocaine. "This is peng innit? It's perfeck!" She moved around the room, turning lights on and off and opening and closing things. Her airport anger now seemed to belong to another dimension, and Olly was pleased—and this pleasure at her happiness acted as a sudden, heavy sedative. He wanted to share his girlfriend's exuberance, but first he needed rest...

"Ya mind if I jus crash?" he asked.

"It's only nine ya pee-stain!" She threw a pillow at him.

"Not in London it aint."

"Idiot. Shoulda slept on the plane. I's gonna explore."

He was asleep before she was even out of the room.

His dreams were the unusual kind brought about by travel, the sudden shift in climate and change of routine plunging him into unfamiliar nocturnal cartographies, and he woke in a sweat caused only partially by the tropical heat. It took him some moments to reorient himself. Daylight was flooding through the open doors of their room and he could hear both the sea and human activity, though nothing distinct in the latter. Sophie was lying naked next to him. She smelt of booze and cigarettes and there was a trail of her clothing leading to the bed. Many men would have been aroused by the scene, but experience had taught Olly that Sophie with a hangover was best left alone. He blinked and found himself pondering the image of a man pushing his erection through the bars of a tiger enclosure. Swipe, snarl. Limp gristle chewed and pawed.

Without waking her he rose and changed into resort-appropriate clothing—a Ralph Lauren swimsuit she'd selected for him, Hawaiian shirt, flip flops—and left the room.

Although it was early, the beach was busy, cluttered with Westerners enjoying their package deals. He could hear familiar accents—Scots, Americans, Germans. The only Thais about were hawking jewellery and knickknacks. He sat in the sand for a moment and removed his shirt, let his skin feel the sun. Sophie liked him tanned, but that was hard to maintain in England without either booking appointments or using a bottle, and both options led to more shit than it was worth taking from his pub mates. Still, after he'd started going out with Sophie they'd been a bit more restrained. While he wasn't fully able to articulate the effects, Olly could tell that her existence in his life had automatically garnered him respect. He was banging a hot girl, and it meant he was a winner—simple as that. Straight up the hierarchy. Suddenly other guys were asking him for advice—not about women, but about entirely unrelated things, like finances. Suddenly they wanted his film and TV recommendations. And sure, being with her had meant a few sacrifices, but he knew that she always had his best interests in mind; what she wanted was to make him a better person. She wanted to help him become the best possible Olly. If that meant waxing his chest, so be it. And he did have to admit to himself that he looked more sculpted without body hair. It was a physique to be proud of, after all—that's what Sophie had said when they'd met—one toned and crafted through hard work and heavy lifting. It was a real man's body, chiselled London granite. Why not make the most out of it?

The sun had warmed his stomach and he could feel new beads of sweat forming at his temples. He tried to remember his dreams. When he couldn't, he stood and moved into the sea, dove forward, swam along the white-sand bottom for as long as he could before his lungs hurt and his face began to tingle and he had to surface. He repeated this process a number of times: deep breath, then under, his arms pulling, his eyes open against the salt until he absolutely had to emerge and suck air. He found the repetition of this act soothing, somehow analogous, but he could not explain why or how.

He explored the area. He looked through the resort's grounds, its tennis courts, the pitch-and-putt golf course, several outdoor bars. A swimming pool teeming with children. He ate breakfast alone at an inexplicably Irish-themed on-site restaurant, then returned to the room.

"Where've ya been?" Sophie asked as he came in. She was sitting on the bed in a sarong and watching TV. She'd recently showered and her hair was wet and combed back.

"Jus gettina know the place," he said. "Ad a swim, some breakfast."

She switched off the screen and looked at him in a way that immediately caused his stomach to hurt. "Ya didn't fink it was a good idea ta wait fa me? I's been sat ere waitin for yas. Now wat the fuck am I spposda do?"

"It's fine," he said. "We'll go togever now. I only ad fruit," he lied.

She seethed at him, mumbled the word inconsiderate, and went into the bathroom.

"So, we goin then?" he called.

"I needa put me makeup on!" Her disembodied anger wafted in from the other room. "Fucken learna fink!"

"Sorry," he heard himself saying. He went to sit

outside and watch the sea.

Over breakfast Sophie made it clear that before anything else she wanted a new series of photos for her various social media feeds. Olly listened and nodded and tried to mentally note her specific visual requests. They'd done this sort of thing a lot, and in many respects he was well trained. He'd come to understand that Sophie suggesting they go to the park actually meant she wanted him to take pictures of her for two hours—pictures with food, pictures of her pouting, pictures of her looking slightly windswept. Not that he minded. He'd come to enjoy the photographic aspects. Artistic endeavour was not something that had been encouraged in his childhood; hammering nails into timber was as close as he'd been allowed to get to creativity without being branded a rainbow-loving mincer. Now he'd discovered that with the right mindset, taking an okay photo of his girlfriend could be personally satisfying. He'd had to suffer through some of her irritation at first (his initial pictures were not masterpieces and she'd critiqued him harshly for misrepresenting her beauty) but with repetition he'd gotten better. He didn't need the lexicon of a professional to take a professional-looking image; composition and lighting became instinctual, and soon Sophie had been genuinely impressed with his work: "This one's real good like! I look like a real model." She'd kiss him, maybe even flirt her hand over his crotch, and they'd return to the task— another photo, this time she's on all fours on the picnic blanket and faux hunting through the basket, subtle cleavage, her dress riding up: gentle titillation before they went home to fuck.

And Olly had known all this during their first day at the resort as Sophie laid out the plans—"I want some inna water, like in the waves"—but he was also struggling to make his way through his second breakfast, a fully cooked bonanza of sausage and egg she'd ordered for him as punishment and which he absolutely knew he had to finish. For herself she'd ordered only fruit and coffee. She finished neither, then lit a cigarette to seal off her appetite. "Jus make me look good, awight."

He nodded his assent and mumbled while trying to swallow.

They took photos on the beach. Twice she called him a faggot. He could sense other people listening, eavesdropping on the mixture of emasculation and homophobia.

Afterwards, once she'd been thoroughly aroused by herself—and, as always, by the wandering gazes of libidinous strangers—they returned to their room to copulate.

From the very beginning of their relationship, sex had been the foundation. He'd frequently lost himself in the raw engine of her body, driven by almost supernatural propulsion to grab her and throw her onto the mattress. And she'd responded to his animalism, the muscular chest, his tattoo, sweat beading off him as he pushed deep. "Leave em aviators on!" she would demand. It made him hot and anonymous, a turgid physical presence swelling over her, and she could watch herself bent and red in the reflection off the lenses. He found himself grabbing at her flesh, and in the early stages she wanted to be savaged, hungered to be thrown around and called names.

Of course, this intensity didn't last. After a few months of high-velocity fucking, things tapered away—returning, he figured, to normal—and before long sex was only a weekend thing, and always after a photo session. Not that he complained; comparatively, he believed, he was still living a life of rich erotic fulfilment. Many of his mates were totally girlfriendless. Some, it seemed, had even resigned themselves to modern celibacy, paying for online porn subscriptions and justifying their choices by claiming £13.99 a month provided more satisfaction and less emotional distress than any real woman.

But they didn't understand the smell of a *real* woman—a tangible body, the twisting eroticism when skin met skin.

Except, as the months passed, Olly found himself more and more superfluous during the process. Eventually, he even came to fear it. Yes, he was in bed with her, but in many ways he might as well have been in the other room watching TV, or at the pub, both of which would have left him with fewer bruises. Her mind seemed to have closed off to him entirely, locking him out of her version of events. And the routine became mechanistic: he was on his back and she would ride him. She would do it theatrically, thumping up and down and whirling and moaning, playing, it appeared, to some ethereal audience.

Then the names began.

Pussy. Idiot. Faggot. Just a few at first. She goaded him to respond. And when he didn't—it wasn't in his nature—out came the slapping and nail-dominated pinchings, the scratching that left deep and bloody marks. Once, she called him a cunt and socked him hard in the jaw, dislodging a molar. Once, she forced him to wear a muzzle.

Today hadn't been so bad. A couple of names and a hard slap, then she'd wrestled an orgasm out of herself and was done…

He looked at her now as she sat beside him at the beach bar, fingering her screen, a mojito placid and cool in front of her. This was his holiday. Here *they* were… He was fading into the middle distance again, unable to articulate his feelings, unable to sort or categorise the toxic miasma.

Muzzle.

He didn't hear the bartender.

"Numpty!" Sophie barked.

"Uh?"

"Guy's talkin ta ya! Daffy cunt." She went back to her phone.

Olly refocused and found the bartender was smiling at him. "Another beer, mate?" The Australian accent was unmistakable. He looked at the bottle in his hand and discovered it was empty, and it occurred to him that he didn't even remember drinking it.

"Cheers."

The bartender popped another one and placed it before Olly, taking care to land a serviette beneath the bottle in a movement that was deft and elegant and put his customer strangely at ease. Olly thanked him and turned back to the sea. The afternoon was settling across the water, lambently hypnotic. Get drunk, he thought. Just get really, really drunk.

"I'm goin back ta the room," Sophie said abruptly, climbing down from her stool, her face stuck to the screen as if by some spell. "Ya finishin ya drink, yeah?" The question seemed cursory, but when he didn't answer she looked up at him briefly.

"Yeah."

"Take ya time," she said. "I'll be in the room. Lata, faggit."

"Bye."

He watched her trail off over the lawn and toward the accommodation, sarong dragging, the soft thacking of her flip-flops fading away. His shoulders loosened—he hadn't realised they were tight. He turned back to his drink.

"Lovely lady," said the bartender.

INT. EXECUTIVE OFFICE – DAY

"Thoughts?" asks the filmmaker. He shifts back in his chair and looks across the desk at the exec.

The exec is tapping his thumbs against each other, but stops before he speaks. "So the shot cuts to the bartender, the audience sees him for the first time—this Australian guy—and it turns out he's the face from the beginning? The one we saw in that very first shot…"

"Exactly."

"And it's going to be absolutely clear to everyone that this is the guy we started with? The man from the opening shot is *one-hundred percent* the bartender. Or is there meant to be some ambiguity?"

"No ambiguity. Although the background will be different, the shot is basically a replica in terms of its framing and the bartender's facial expression—remember the slight disgust? It's also going to hang on him for a bit.

The only way the audience won't make the connection is if they missed the opening to buy popcorn or are in the throes of a cerebral haemorrhage."

"I like it," the exec says. "It leads to questions. Good questions. How will this guy be connected? Whose phone is he on? And the speculations are sinister. I'm thinking sex and death, and I'm liking it."

"Good. How about the rest—you're still in the flow with me? You're happy?"

The exec pauses for a moment, creates a loose fist out of his right hand and moves it up to cover his mouth. He then looks up in the corner of the room as his brow enters a ruminative, semi-furrowed state. The filmmaker waits, content that honest intellectual processing is taking place. Eventually the exec removes his hand from his mouth and returns his focus. "Okay," he says. "First I'm going to comment on some of the things I'm liking specifically. Then I'm going to comment on things I have questions about, bearing in mind that at this stage these questions—both narrative and aesthetic—may be answered later in the piece."

"Shoot."

"Firstly, I love the visual presentation of Olly's backstory. Without voiceover and with multiple layered flashbacks, that's incredibly difficult to do, but I think you've more than nailed it. *And* you've done it without being heavy-handed. Really deft touch."

"How did you feel about the underwater reverse-tracking shot?"

The exec answers without the slightest hesitation. "I think it's brave to make that a minute long. But that's also a real payoff in terms of meaning. I like that kind of filmmaking."

"And you get that he's, you know, holding his breath in his own life, that he's sort of drowning on a day-to-day basis?"

"I think it's clear."

"But it's not too clear? I'm not bludgeoning people to death with it?"

"Look, Max, you know this, but I'm going to reassure you anyway. There's no right way to do this kind of thing—it's a bit of a guessing game. You get a film critic who's spent their entire miserable life picking these things apart and to them pretty much everything is hackneyed and obvious. They professionally study filmic architecture and pathologically hunt for symbols, and as soon as they find them they sandbag you. The only way to impress viewers like that is to cast all the pieces randomly and let them find meaning for themselves. But you've got to remember, the audience we're after are the ones who watch films to watch films. They don't automatically see the structure—they don't want to. And when a symbol is pointed out to them, they gasp at the genius."

"You're right."

"I *am* right. And I'll tell you, the underwater sequence: magnificent. Explain that shit to one of the plebs in the back of the theatre and they'll cream their jeans. And that's another thing: keep that sex coming. The reflection off the aviator lenses: hot. Love it. Makes me hard thinking about it, and this girl's totally imaginary." The exec breaks off for a moment and appears to enter a steamy reverie.

"How about your questions?" the filmmaker asks.

The exec draws himself out of his imagination and back into the room. "Sophie," he says. "The girl. I'm wondering whether she's being painted a shade too black at this stage… Of course, I don't know what's coming, so I'm just floating this out there and I'll leave it to you as to whether you think this needs to be confronted yet."

"What worries you specifically?" While the filmmaker's face does not strictly convey concern, his expression is teetering on the edge of it.

"I guess what I'm asking is whether she's going to stay a two-dimensional antagonist or whether she's going to evolve, and I guess that really has to do with what her overall function in the narrative will be. I know there's still a lot I don't know."

The filmmaker can't help asking. "You think she's two-dimensional?"

"We just know more about Olly than we do about her at this stage. In terms of characterisation we get that she's mean, selfish, vain and likes to slap around her boyfriend while sliding on his knob, but…"

"What?"

"To avoid the misogyny label you might have to give her a backstory—and shit, stop me if there's one on its way, but you really need to find some hidden ameliorating trauma, show why she is the way she is. Or something that *explains*, at least. It doesn't have to excuse." The exec can see that the filmmaker is no longer bordering concern; he's becoming annoyed instead.

"Can't some people just be shitty because they're shitty? Why do we have to find reasons for it all the time?"

"That's totally fine. We just need to pay lip service to motivation. It might simply be that she's a cunt because she comes from a family richly populated with the cunt gene. It's just important to slide that moment into the film."

"Look, I'm just arguing this from a theoretical point of view." The filmmaker's irritation fades and he becomes confident again. "Don't worry about Sophie, she's not just a MacGuffin—she gets plenty of space to grow. And you're not going to see it coming. Should be a mind blower."

The exec sits back in his chair and redeploys his index-finger isosceles. "That's a big call, my friend. But I'm excited. Now, where were we?"

"The bartender has become a character, as indicated by the last shot, and Olly has decided to get drunk—lending us the opportunity to introduce a visual signature to the film via a carefully crafted drinking montage."

The exec smiles and does his little pointing thing. "Hit me."

INT. DELUXE DOUBLE SUITE - NIGHT

Eleanor Murphy was watching the TV and watching her husband—who was also watching the TV—and watching her kids as she sat on the lounge in their suite. It was the fifth day of their package-deal holiday and it seemed, by the time night fell, that they no longer had the motivation for local curiosities or prefabricated tourist activities. Instead, they had decided to spend the evening engaged in one of the wiser and more globally accepted traditions of American cultural hegemony, ordering pizza to their room and watching a movie. Now Eleanor was lamenting the fact she'd let Mike choose the film, given his tendency to select based on weirdness or perceived level of viewing challenge. But she also knew that if she kicked up a loud enough fuss before the end of the first act, she had a shot at changing it. "I don't understand this," she said.

On the bed on the far side of the suite her twins

giggled at something—giggling the way six-year-olds do. Eleanor had got herself out of the habit of asking what was funny. She'd been disappointed by the inanities of her children too often and had all but given up expecting sparks of genius or callow elements of wonder. Invariably what was funny was simply that the table was green, or, worse, something totally nonsensical, like *sticky is moomoo*. Just once she wanted a sharp observation:

What's funny?

The relentless indifference of the cosmos, mother.

She sighed. She wasn't genuinely bored by them, of course. She loved them. And as kids went, they seemed psychologically sound and happy in the way all parents are meant to hope for.

"What don't you understand?" Mike said, not turning his face from the screen. "This is meant to be a classic."

"Just because it's a classic doesn't mean it's easy to understand, or that it's any good. *Salò's* a classic and it's got naked children eating shit from a trough."

"Look, *you* let me choose."

"And you chose poorly. You're the Nazi collaborator at the end of *The Last Crusade*. May you age at an accelerated rate and explode in a cloud of bone dust." The twins giggled again. "See, they find it funny."

"They're not laughing at you." Mike leaned around. "Boys, what are you laughing at?"

Jason—who was older by a minute—held up a chess piece from a set Mike had reluctantly bought from a hawker on the beach. It appeared to be a knight. "It's a horsey," he said.

"Good boy," Mike replied.

"Look, that doesn't change the fact I don't understand what's going on."

"That's because you're talking."

She hit Mike with one of the lavender throw pillows. "*You* don't understand what's going on."

"Yes, I do. I've got a full grasp of the story so far. There was a planet-face thing, then a kind of sperm thing came out of a mouth and drifted about for a while. Now this guy with the stupid haircut is walking around. It's gripping."

At this point Eleanor knew she'd won. Mike making fun of the entertainment signalled that it had gone terminal as a viewing experience. Still, she wanted to let him make the move to end it. If he thought it was his decision, he'd ultimately be happier. She tucked her legs up onto the lounge so her knees rested under her chin and watched the screen as the protagonist carried shopping through an industrial wasteland.

"Alright," Mike said. "I've had enough. Let's watch something else."

"You're very smart and attractive."

He ignored her and began searching around himself for the remote control, then stood up to look under the cushion.

"Mommy," Matthew said.

"Yes, dear?"

"There is people shouting."

She turned to find her younger son peeking through the curtains of the room. "Say that again, my love?"

"There is people shouting."

"Got it!" Mike looked at the remote for a moment as if it were the chief spoil of an archaeological dig, then switched the film off. "What's he babbling about?"

But without the ambience of the T.V. they could both hear: it was muffled by the double-glazed, noise-dampening windows, sure, but there were most certainly voices outside, their volume turned all the way up to Hate-Scream.

"Think the outbreak's begun?" Eleanor asked. "Bleeding eyeballs, hectic cannibalism."

"Don't scare the children please." Mike was already moving to his son. "Come on, buddy, away from there—let me have a look." He took Matthew by the shoulders and shifted him paternally to the bed.

"Good thing we're on the second floor," Eleanor continued. "We should block the stairway and jam the elevator. How are our food supplies?" But her husband wasn't listening. "Mike? What's going on? What's happening?" She turned herself around and leaned over the back of the lounge. "What is it?"

"It's a couple. They're really going at it, too."

"Oh! Let me see!" She jumped up and moved instinctually to her sons, who were sitting in a rather docile fashion on the bed. "Come on, lovelies, over to the sofa." Taking one hand from each she tugged them away, flicked on the TV again, and raced to join her husband, inserting herself next to him in the gap between the curtains.

The Murphys entered the scene *in media res*: on the lawn below, a muscular guy in shorts and flip-flops was holding his arms out in a way that suggested he didn't know what he'd done. He had a footballer's haircut and an unmistakable dumbness about him. The shouting didn't suit his face, but he was doing it anyway, bellowing something hoarse and incoherent. In front of him, but with her back to the gawping parents on the second floor, was a slim woman in a very tight strapless dress and platform shoes. On outfit alone, one might have assumed she was going clubbing. The most noticeable feature about her appearance, however, was the wooden chair she was brandishing above her head. Intermittently she jerked forward with it, her skinny arms quivering with rage as she threatened to bash the guy, and he seemed to be leaning in, wilfully exposing himself and daring her to do it. She too was screaming incoherently.

"What do you make of this?" Mike said. They were both still hunkered against the curtains.

"He has a magnificent chest," Eleanor said.

"Wax?"

"Almost certainly."

Mike scratched his chin. The guy seemed to be barking, or mimicking a dog. "They look like reality TV stars."

"Maybe they are." Eleanor tried to get her face closer to the glass, although her forehead was already pressed against it. "Open the window a bit. I wanna hear them."

As soon as Mike cracked the seal the screaming took on a whole new dimension. Along with the hot night air, in rushed an obscenity-soaked torrent of working class English abuse, the noise in the red, and at first the sheer scale of the fight and the tangle of language rendered it impervious to analysis, impossible to decipher. The two were shouting right over each other in a garbled, slang-heavy cacophony of pointed syllables that made them sound more like jungle animals that human beings. The guy was drunk—that much was clear. Mike thought it was a point worth making.

"Or brain damaged," Eleanor replied.

"Honey, please."

The fight continued, the woman jerking forward and threatening again, then suddenly the guy seemed to take a breath, leaving the woman space to articulate something clearly enough for the Murphys to understand.

"What did she just say?" Mike asked.

"She said, Fuck off you gimpy fuck-mook. Then she called him a faggot."

"Get your phone. This needs recording."

Eleanor ducked back inside the suite and hunted for her Samsung. It was on the table next to the sofa. The twins were watching the TV, which was once again playing *Eraserhead*. She plugged in her passcode and fumbled through the functions, trying to find the video camera.

"Mommy."

"Just a moment, dear." She couldn't find the app.

"What's a fuck-mook?"

Found it. She was on and recording. "A type of racoon, honey." She raced back to the window with the phone outstretched, focusing down on the couple just in time to catch the blow.

"Wow, Jesus!" Mike blurted. The woman had really gone for it with the chair, catching the guy on the head with one of the legs; it made a donk sound against his skull and broke off. "Is this the point we say something?" The guy was holding his head, mixing shouts and moans in a way that didn't leave anyone with dignity.

"You could call the front desk?" Eleanor was fixed on the screen of her camera, determined to miss nothing.

"Surely someone else has done that already. We can't be the only ones watching this." Mike took a deeper breath and felt his heart beat faster. He didn't like involving himself in confrontations. It wasn't his style. But in this case it seemed like it had to be done. He stood up and opened the curtains as wide as they would go and pushed the window completely open, hoping his elevated platform might give him a natural impression of authority, like an emperor watching gladiators—*all I have to do is invert my thumb and you'll be fed to the lions.* "Excuse me," he called.

The couple ignored him.

"You might want to go for a bolder approach," his wife suggested. She'd shuffled to the side of the window in a way that left her largely out of sight.

He turned to her. "Do *you* want to do this?"

"I had to give birth."

"Ya like that ya fucken faggit!"

Now Mike had his entry point. "Hey! Lady, we've got kids up here! Hey!"

As the woman turned her head Mike had the sensation of being engulfed by a totally foreign force; no amount of lipstick or eyeliner could hide how feral her expression was. "Wat!?" Her accent acted like a blunt weapon.

Mike persevered. "You think this might be something you and your boyfriend could take somewhere else? Or alternatively maybe you could both calm down? I'd prefer my kids didn't have to see this."

She shot straight back: "Mine-ya own fucken business ya fucken yank cunt!"

Mike swallowed. "Look, I can see that you're a reasonable and sophisticated woman, so I'm sure you'll respect that I'm asking you nicely. We do in fact have kids up here, and at the moment you're not only teaching them to swear but you're teaching them about the vulgarity of British culture, so do you…–"

"Why'd you stop?" Eleanor asked, still angling her phone out at the lawn. "You're doing really well."

"She's gone back inside," Mike said. "Seems they're staying underneath us. The guy's still out here, though."

"I can hear him. If he wasn't brain damaged before he might be now."

"Honey. Decorum. Oh wait, here she is!"

Eleanor no longer felt the need to hide. She pulled herself into the window light and watched with her husband as the woman stormed back out onto the lawn and made a beeline for the darkness of the beachfront. The guy, still clutching his head, tried a clumsy grab for her, but she dodged him without effort and charged ahead.

"Thank you!" called Mike. "It's been a pleasure!"

Before reaching the shadows, the woman made a point of turning and flicking him off and shouting one final obscenity: "Cockface!"

"Bitch!" It was Eleanor this time, flaring out into the darkness. But the woman was already in the night shadows, moving under the palm trees and heading for the shore.

In the light beneath them the guy continued to clutch his head. He'd ceased shouting, although it had been substituted with noticeable groans, and he was moving in confused circles that reminded Eleanor of wildlife footage. "Hey, buddy," she called. "You okay?"

"Doesn't look it," Mike said.

"Hey. Are you okay?"

Instead of answering, the guy looked toward the light of what the Murphys presumed was his own room, then wandered into it, ignoring them completely and disappearing from view.

Mike left the window and picked up the suite's phone. "You calling the front desk?" his wife asked.

He nodded at the same time as someone picked up. The voice was Australian: "Front desk. How can I help?"

"Hi there. I'd just like to report, well, I guess a disturbance? And I think one of your guests might need some medical attention."

Eleanor watched her husband on the phone as he laid things out. She looked over at the TV. The twins seemed to be enjoying the film a lot more than she had. It was a dinner scene—the character with the funny haircut was trying to carve a cooked chicken, but it was moving around on his plate. The boys were giggling.

"Thanks," Mike said. "That's really kind of you. Thanks again. Bye." He hung up. "Well, that's fantastic."

"What? Are they sending someone to check if he's okay?"

"Yep. But get this: we're getting two days of our stay refunded, and from now on all our food and drink is complimentary."

"You're kidding?" Eleanor found herself flooded by inconceivable joy.

"Dead serious." Mike smiled.

"You hear that, boys?" The twins twisted their heads away from the TV; both were grinning and had the demeanour and cuteness of meerkats. "Because mommy and daddy stuck their noses into other people's business, we're all getting things for free! What do you think about that?"

They returned their attention to the movie without answering her. The man with the funny hair had managed to skewer his twitching chicken, although it had started screaming horrifically and was spurting globs of blood all over the plate.

INT. EXECUTIVE OFFICE – DAY

"I thought you said we were going to learn more about the Australian guy," the exec says.

The filmmaker smiles. "Double blind, right?"

"I don't think it's necessary to trick me. You're meant to be pitching."

"Look, let me sell this the way I want to sell it. It's all part of the patchwork that makes the quilt," he says with assurance. "All threads are necessary. To tell a really good story it's sometimes important to displace the audience and hide what the story is. It helps them focus. You want me to continue?"

"Sure."

"So now it's late morning—we can tell by the quality of the light—and the camera's looking at a ceiling fan, and it's thrupping…"

"Thrupping?"

"Whirling and thrupping. Think *Apocalypse Now*."

INT. INDETERMINATE – MORNING

Olly lay on his back, unsure where he was, only half sure *who* he was. He could hear the sounds of a lawnmower, or a helicopter—it was difficult to tell. He was sweating badly, and the light had a flickering sharpness that hurt his eyes. Where was he? He had no physical notion of his context. If he'd been asked what country he was in, the answer would not have come to him. He could sense his nudity. What had happened to his clothing? And now he was having trouble getting up, difficultly with the fundamentals of rising; it was like his arms were still asleep. He had to strain his stomach and crunch his abdominals to get forward and pull himself into a sitting position, but even then the room refused to become any clearer, lost in a hologram of fog. He tried to turn himself, but the movement was awkward and off balance. Then he discovered why. His arms had been neatly severed. They lay behind him like bloodless butchery meat. He screamed and looked down to discover he was also missing his penis. In its place was a coagulated wound.

His eyes were open.

A ceiling fan was thrupping and whirling directly above him, pulsing air across his body. I'm awake, he thought. I'm awake. He shifted his arms and felt for his dick, and the confirmation that everything was intact calmed him immensely. Only after penile certainly had been established could other existential inquiries be tackled… A man awakes to find himself floating inexplicably in a dimensional void and that he has no penis. His first question is never about the void.

The ceiling fan was thrupping. Thrupping.

He was on holiday.

He was in Thailand.

He tried to find the last thing in his memory. The beach. Photos. Sex. A slap in the face. They came back to him jagged and epileptic, foaming flashes of colour. Sophie's voice.

Thrupping.

He didn't remember his room having a ceiling fan.

He sat up suddenly, but the movement went to work on his brain in ways he was not prepared for—the whole thing felt swollen and clumsy, full of volatile fluids. "Easy, fella," a voice said. "No sense in rushing things." Olly tried to turn and find the speaker, but focusing on anything beyond his immediate pain was not an option. His mouth was dry and tasted like toilet. "You had yourself a big night. Remember much of it?" Olly shook his head, then grabbed it with both hands to try and halt the swirling agony. "Took a bit of a knock there, mate." He closed his eyes tight and tried to squeeze away the pain. When he opened them again, the voice had become a face. Some guy was squatting down in front of him, forcing a water bottle into his hand and offering him pills. "You remember who I am?" Olly tried to say no, but had difficulty. "You sure? Don't remember my face at all? Nothing? Zippo…?" The guy was non-descript—just a guy—although the Australian accent was unmissable. "That's a shame. I like to think of myself as someone who makes an impression. Guess not."

Olly took a drink of water. He found swallowing hard, and when he spoke, his voice came out raspy and barely audible. "Where am I?" He sounded like an old man.

"You, matey-moo, are currently situated in one of the resort's luxury beachfront cabins. Lucky for you you're on the inside with major players like myself…You *sure* you don't remember me?" The guy raised an eyebrow.

"Sorry, mate."

"After all we've been through. Scandalous." The Aussie stood up and started moving about the room, although Olly didn't have the will or inclination to keep track of what he was doing. "So you don't even remember my name…?"

Blank space. Vacuum. The room was still pulsing; it felt as if the walls were moving in an out in time to the sound of the fan. He wondered if something in his brain had broken. The guy was still talking, still saying things, but the words were falling away like crumbly earth. "Where's Sophie?" he found himself asking.

"Ah, your delightful other half. You stabbed her to death because she was a huge bitch and she was ruining your life."

"Wat?"

The Aussie looked back at Olly very seriously, just long enough to see the insanity he was generating, before reverting to a smile. "Sorry, mate. You're not in any state to be fucked with. That was cruel of me." He took a seat on a chair next to the bed and put his hands in his lap, and for the first time Olly registered the blue polo shirt uniform of the resort's staff. "Sophie's fine. Let's start from the beginning, shall we? I'm Jack. I work here. We met yesterday at, oh…" He moved to look at a watch that didn't exist, then back up…"about twenty-two hours ago. And what a ride it's been since then. What a whirlwind relationship we have had!" Jack grinned at Olly for a moment, letting it all hang there, and Olly had an odd sensation—one that cut through his pain and disorder— that a butterfly was somehow being mutilated, that its wings were being chopped up with scissors.

Jack continued: "So, around two o'clock postmeridian yesterday I was tending one of the resort's finer drinking establishments when you and old Soph wandered in. You both sat there like tragic lumps for a bit—good looking lumps, mind you—and then your girly-girl got up and left, and it very quickly became apparent that you were planning a full-blown expedition to Drunksville. One beer led to another, then you were doing shots, and pretty soon everything got loose. Of course, we got to talking, as happens in any good bartender-customer relationship. Frankly, mate, I felt we shared things—important things. You told me all about the Sophinator, the bedroom issues, your deeper feelings about power and masculinity, and I told you my name.

"Anyway, by the time the long shadows were casting themselves over the beach you were eating your own shit. It was *inhuman*, baby. You're a real monster, you know that? But I kinda felt responsible for the state you were in since I'd been serving you the drinks…Any of this jogging the noggin?" Olly shook his head.

Frames missing.

Pages torn out.

"Wow. Okay, so at this point, largely because I'm a conscientious fellow and an excellent listener, I thought maybe it wasn't a great idea to send you back to your love interest in such a state, and given my shift was finishing—and maybe because I didn't want my supervisor to see that I'd let you turn yourself inside out—I took you down to the beach to cool off for a bit, figuring that if you had a swim you'd either sober up or drown." Jack grinned at Olly. Olly blinked at Jack. "Anyhow, after you'd had a bit of a splash you seemed a bit more temperate and I reckoned I could leave you out there on the sand. The sun was setting, things were calm, and you were looking nicely toasted. The pink sky, mate! The waves! All that shit's a real tranquilizer.

"Have ya noticed what a great storyteller I am?—I feel I'm putting all the right paints on the canvas here.

"Anyway, once I knew you were enjoying a wee visit from the sandman I wandered back to the resort to continue with the rest of my life—stopping, mind you, to politely inform the charming Soph that you were out on the beach and would be back presently. And may I just add that she did not seem particularly concerned." Jack broke off and got up and started whistling with a chipper nonchalance. Then he left the room.

"That it?" Olly called, his voice gravel.

The sound of a strong stream of urine hitting toilet water. The sound of a flushing toilet.

Jack returned and sat back down. "I know," he said. He went serious again, his expression morbidly blank. "Didn't wash my hands. I'm not a nice person." He leaned in closer to Olly and dropped into a conspiratorial whisper: "Once, I popped this kid's balloon just to see the little pussy cry about it. I'm a total nihilist." His face reverted to the tenebrous smile that seemed to be its natural position. "Now, the next few hours are really anyone's guess. I know what *I* was doing, but I can't say for sure what *you* were doing. I do, however, have my suspicions. My guess is that you awoke from your slumber not long after my departure and wandered down along the main strip, drinking and taking whatever crazy chemicals lurked into your circumference. Fair dinkum?"

"Wat?"

Jack put his hands on his knees and leaned forward. "Ya like drugs, Olly? Ya seem like you probably enjoy a drug or two." He leaned back and held his palms up. "None of my business, obviously—we all indulge in something. My mum, for example, mainlined Jesus. But in your case, it's likely material to our grip on the missing fragments of the story. My guess is you continued to ply yourself with whatever came your way along The Strip—ketamine, amphetamine, voodoo—and then you came back, well after dark, and we had the opportunity to dance together all over again. You got ya phone on you per chance?"

"Why?" Olly felt around himself and discovered he was lying on it.

"Just curious," Jack continued. "You get any messages from Sophie today? Or last night? When was the last time she checked in?" Jack suddenly looked worried, which worried Olly.

He opened WhatsApp—it was all they used. The last message had been the night before. 21.05: 'Fuckstick where are you I'm in the room'.

"Anything?" Jack asked.

"One last night. Bout nine."

"What's it say?"

Right then a wave of self-consciousness overcame Olly, and with it the sense that his essential privacy was being violated. He felt he was starting to come back to himself, and this guy—this lippy Australian in a polo shirt—was being extremely invasive. Who the hell was he anyway? "Look, mate, I'm sorry, but I don't fink this is any of ya business. Jeknow wat I mean?"

Jack lost his look of concern, leaned back calmly, and returned to the macabre grinning that seemed to be his status quo. He folded his right leg over his left and looked at Olly in silence. Then, very casually, he removed something red from his pocket and took a crunching bite from it—an apple. He chewed. He took another bite, the fruit noisy and wet inside the cavern of his mouth.

Olly's brain was hurting again. "Sorry," he found himself saying. Having had its wings diced, the butterfly's legs were now being pulled off. After that there would remain only a thorax, wiggling antennae… "I'm just…"

Jack finished his mouthful. "Look mate, I'm here for ya. You've gotta understand that even though you don't know me, I already know you. And I fully appreciate that cryptic crosswords aren't your kind of thing. But you're *good looking*—and that counts for a lot in this world. Now we're just trying to piece all this together, so what did the message say?"

Olly found himself complying: "She was asking wheres I was."

"Okay then. So, I guess after your hunt for cocaine and ping-pong chickadees you must have got the message and staggered back here. At this point we've got a confirmed record of your whereabouts. Do you wanna guess what happened next?"

He found himself touching his head tenderly, feeling the lump and its parameters for the first time. He closed his eyes and felt like crying. "Did I 'it 'er?"

"Shit, mate, what a dark avenue to veer into. I worry about some of the impulses you've got swimming around in there. But, no. *She hit you*—that's right, that's the lump. Broke a chair over you, wrestling style."

"A chair?"

"Some more respectable guests saw the whole thing from their room."

Then Olly really did start crying. He couldn't help it, big goofy sobs convulsing out of him: he'd ruined his holiday; his girlfriend hated him; his head hurt.

Jack watched the Englishman as if he were a specimen, as if he were a lab animal being exposed to malicious chemicals. "You right there, matey-moo? Need a hanky?" He retrieved one from his pocket and thrust it at him. The convulsions continued. "You're snotting on that chest of yours… Look, mate, hey—over here." He waited until Olly peered up from his mucus. "Everything's fine. Nothing's broken. Luckily I was on the desk last night, so it was me who took the calls about the disturbance. I came over, found you in a right state, and decided—judiciously, if I do say so myself—to put you in here and give you and your lady some space from each other. Now, I want you to listen to me here. Are you listening?"

Olly nodded through his curtain of sobs.

"In the interests of harmony and happiness, I'd like you to stay in this room today. I've comped all your food, so order anything you want. Maybe stay away from the booze—but I'm not your mum, so whatever. As for

Sophie, I've given her tickets for a moped tour up the coast, so she'll be out of here soon, and depending on how she feels she could be gone for the night. Now, I'm no relationship counsellor—I've had a more intimate relationship with that hanky you're wiping your face with than most of the women in my life—but your girlfriend is a horrible fucking bitch and you'd be better off without her. Can I suggest you dwell on that today? And for god's sake, whatever you do, don't message her with any bullshit about your feelings." Jack stood up and took another bite of his apple, chewed it and looked toward the door. "Last thing—and this might help clear some of the logistical barriers to the freeing of your Johnson and your tiny wee ego: if you do decide you don't ever want to see her again, you can have this cabin through to the end of your stay, no extra charge. I can also pull strings and get you on different flights home."

Olly's sobbing was easing back. "Fanks," he mumbled. In the barrage of it all, someone else was making sense for him. Someone else was catching and ordering the toxic fog.

"Harmony and happiness," Jack repeated. "Call the front desk if you need me—*Jack*, remember. *Jack*, *Jack*, *Jack*. And keep the hanky—she was good to me, but all things come to an end."

Then Olly was alone.

INT. EXECUTIVE OFFICE – DAY

"Want lunch?" the exec asks. "We could order something in, or we could go out for a change of scene?"

"I like it here," says the filmmaker. "I feel we're establishing a mood."

"What are you after? Any particular cravings we can sate?"

The filmmaker thinks for a second. "I'll have exactly the same thing you're having—even if it's live octopus. And if you can't decide between two things, get both and when they arrive I'll have the one you don't want."

"Excellent." The exec hits the intercom on his desk to signal his assistant, and following a momentary buzzing a voice appears.

"Yes, sir?"

"Hi, Benny. Could we get some food ordered in please? Could I have some Thai-style beef noodles—in one of those New York cartons if possible. You know the ones I mean. And could I also have a wide selection of dim sum?"

"The Chinese dumplings, sir?"

"Yes, Benny."

"Anything to drink with that, sir?"

"Two beers, please. Although make sure it's Thai beer. That okay?"

"Of course, sir. I'll send out for it now."

"Thanks." The executive lets go of the intercom and feels it's necessary to comment on his assistant's efficiency. "Kid's amazing. I could ask for a cup of virgin's blood and he'd have it here within the hour."

"It's hard to find good people these days."

"Not if you pay them enough." The exec smiles. "So, the dream sequence with the missing dick and arms: great. It destabilizes the audience."

"Just enough to keep them actively watching, right?"

"I like the inclusion of nightmare body horror as well. Even if it's taking place in a dream scenario, it's opening that possibility for the viewer."

The filmmaker readjusts himself in his seat. "That was my feeling. Dream or not, once a notion that extreme has entered the diegesis, it's there as potential for the rest of the film. You can't *un*-see it, so you sort of expect more."

The exec is nodding. He pushes his Portuguese office chair back from the desk and spins a slow three-sixty degrees, his left index finger patting his lips in thought. He has not finished his full rotation, but begins speaking anyway. "I love what you're thinking with those flashbacks, too—using the Aussie's description as a guide. I know that's standard flashback practice, but it's more to do with the images you've selected as Olly's new memories. They open up the possibility of new settings for the viewer. They help *grow* the film." The exec taps his fingers sequentially against his desk before pointing at the filmmaker. "That voodoo section with the goat's testicles is particularly inspired—gory, but it works. And the ping pong show is a nice touch: keeps the promise of sex right there. Dirty sex, too. Immoral. Because that stuff's all tied up with sex tourism and Western exceptionalism. It's unhygienic, unethical depravity. I like it. Makes me think of Polanski... You ever been to a ping pong show?"

"Fraid not," says the filmmaker.

The exec loses himself in contemplation again and for a moment there is silence in the room. The filmmaker can hear traffic beyond the walls of the building and the sound of a phone ringing in another office.

"You think that's something I can bother my wife with?"

"What, taking her to a show? Probably have a hard time finding one outside South-East Asia."

"No, I mean getting her to try it herself."

"Well, I don't know your wife. I guess it depends on the type of relationship you have with her. Is there any harm in asking?"

The exec taps the knuckle of his middle finger against

the edge of his desk and bites his bottom lip. "There might be…" He remains still and unfocused for a moment, then looks back up at the filmmaker, having retrieved himself from the fuzzy cushion of thought. "You want to test something out?"

"Not if it involves ping pong balls. We haven't even had lunch."

The exec laughs and presses the intercom again. "I've told you how much I like your sense of humour, right?" The intercom buzzes, then Benny's voice comes through, crisp and ready.

"Yes, sir?"

"Has lunch been ordered, Benny?"

"Already on its way, sir."

"Great. Next thing, and this might prove a bit of a challenge, I was wondering if you could find me a cup of virgin's blood—by which I mean a cup of blood from a virgin…"

There is a very short pause before Benny replies. "Is this a serious request, sir?"

"Yes, Benny. Is that a problem?"

"Of course not, sir. I just have a couple of questions to facilitate the process."

"Go ahead."

"Would you like a metric cup or an imperial cup?"

"I'm normally into a C-cup, but let's go metric on this one."

"Very good, sir. And when would you like to have it?"

"ASAP."

"Okay. In terms of budget, how much leeway is there?"

"No more than, hmm…" The exec takes his finger off the intercom and speaks to the filmmaker: "I hadn't thought about that." The filmmaker shrugs, signalling that blood price is not his area of expertise. The exec pushes the button back down. "Let's say no more than $750."

"And would you like some certification to ensure the blood's virginal authenticity?"

"Your assurance will be fine, Benny."

"And just one last thing, sir—how would you like the product presented: vacuum sealed in a medical bag, or in a looser more accessible form?"

"Surprise me."

"Thank you, sir. You should have it by early this afternoon."

"You're magic, Benny." The exec takes his finger off the intercom and looks at the filmmaker. "Kid's ivy league. My bet is he comes in well underbudget."

EXT. BEACH FRONT – LATE MORNING

Thirty-six hours had passed since the Murphy family had been granted free and unfettered access to the resort's food and drink resources, and in the intervening period they had been making the most of it. On the morning after the initial disturbance, their room resembled a culinary atrocity, strewn with pizza crusts, prawn tails and half-finished sundaes. In the orgy of consumption little Jason had puked on himself, and Matthew—due largely to his habit of seasoning his meals with whatever he excavated from the carpet—had enjoyed an energetic bout of excessively liquid faeces. Regardless, the gorging continued into the next day, with big breakfasts, four-course lunches, and an evening meal in the more refined of the resort's two restaurants—the one designed as a facsimile of French sophistication and strategically priced beyond the range of most normal travelling families. Mike wore his best Acapulco shirt, Eleanor a T-shirt with an image of zombies devouring the face of the American president. They ordered expensive wine, dishes that were difficult to prepare, and their children were noisy enough to annoy other guests. "To winning at life!" Eleanor said, raising her glass at her husband while her son knocked his Coca-Cola on the floor.

Yet by eleven a.m. the following day, Mike had fallen into an emotional trench. He was eating nachos off his chest (*sans* bowl) and reclining in a sun lounger that had been carried to the beach for him by an obsequious employee—just the right kind of obsequious: fawning, servile; brimming with token compliments that confirmed Mike's choices were definitely the *best* choices. The sun was warming his stomach. Cheese and sour cream were caught in his chest hair. He was holding a cold beer and watching his twin boys build sandcastles beside the lucid waters of a tropical beach. And yet he felt unequivocally dysphoric. He felt bored.

"Hedonic treadmill," Eleanor said after he'd tried to explain his sense of personal distress. She too was recumbent in a sun lounger; with her sunglasses on it was difficult to tell if she was asleep or awake. A bottle of iced champagne lay nestled in the sand beside her, though she was quite happy to let it go flat and throw it away. "You've had too much of a good thing, and now you've adjusted to a new level of opulent living. The only way to feel good again is to crank up the voltage. You need to get to the next level of debauchery."

"Eat nachos off my chest in a sex club?"

"Or develop at taste for human flesh. Or you could mix both. Up to you, honey; it's your treadmill."

Mike dipped a nacho in the increasingly tepid mound of sour cream on his left nipple and put it in his mouth, although he didn't have the impetus to chew. A German couple shuffled by on the sand in front of him and tried not to look. He turned to Eleanor and spoke with the nacho still in his mouth, but the words came out thick and garbled.

"Sorry, dear?"

Mike let the soggy corn chip drop from his orifice and into the sand. "I said, how come *you're* not on the treadmill?"

"I am. I just metabolise pleasure at a different rate. A more psychologically evolved rate."

"How long do you think you have?"

"Until I need to level up? I could probably keep this rate with ample enjoyment for another few days; after that I think we should kill the children and get down to drug-party sex tourism."

"That's all well and good, but what am I supposed to do until then?"

"In the short term you could pour me a glass of bubbly." Mike sat up and let his food—the medley of nachos, chopped tomato, guacamole and sour cream—tumble down off his chest in a slimy Tex-Mex landslide that came to rest on his crotch. "You're a stylish man," Eleanor said.

He poured some champagne into his wife's glass, letting it foam right over the rim and his greased-up fingers. He could feel the moist weight of cheesy kibble still dangling from individual chest hairs as he looked down the beach. "Speaking of elegance," he said.

"What?"

"Look who it is…" He nodded toward the water.

His wife lifted her head to see, having to tense the muscles of her neck in the process; she was on the verge of complaining about the unnecessary exertion when she spotted the guy. "Oh, yeah. That's him, right?"

"That's our man: big chest, ugly tattoo. Drifting look of bewilderment."

Eleanor pulled herself into a sitting position and lifted her sunglasses. The guy was standing calf-deep in the waters of the foreshore and squinting intently at his phone. "Any sign of Fatal Attraction?" she asked.

"The girl? Not that I can see. I wouldn't call her Fatal Attraction though. Do you want this?" Mike held out the champagne glass; Eleanor took it.

"Why not? She didn't look like a Fatal Attraction to you?"

Mike pulled off some of the cheese stuck in his body hair and toyed with putting it in his mouth. "Not to me, no." Into his mouth it went.

"Don't you think you're setting your standards a little high there, buddy?"

"I think you've misunderstood me, my dear. Her appearance isn't the issue. Both her and doofus over there belong to that plasticine one percent whose cartoonish good looks are almost—not quite, I hasten to add—but *almost* a disability. No, by Fatal Attraction I assume you mean she's a *femme fatale*, and *femme fatales* are more than just physical sex appeal. It's a prerequisite for them to have style, culture, and sophistication. If you want to convince a sleazy lawyer to murder your husband before you set him up to take the fall, you really have to know which one the dessert spoon is. And you heard her—what was it, Fuckmook? She had all the class of a dick pic."

"Point taken." Eleanor sipped her drink and pursed her lips. "This tastes like nacho. Did you wash your hands with it and catch the runoff in the glass?" She held her drink up to the light: "There's salsa floating in it!"

But Mike was still watching the guy, still studying his movement. "Look at him: he's trying to get a signal. Oh, wait, no, back to the screen. That's my boy, stare blankly at the screen again for a while you poor mollusc."

Eleanor ditched the glass and silently resolved to get a whole new bottle. Given the slovenly dissolution into which they'd sunk, there was little point in pursuing culpability—there would be no point in a hearing or a trial: not in these decadent final days of the republic, she thought. Who could judge his fellow man in this season of sin? Who could honestly lay claim to a banner untarnished by wickedness or lasciviousness?

"You think he's trying to contact her?" Mike asked. "Imagine being stuck with someone that horrible. How does that happen?" He dug a mixture of guacamole and tomato out of his bellybutton with his index finger and held it up in the sunlight.

"It just happens," Eleanor said. She looked over toward the twins, who remained busy carefully constructing their sandcastle. Even from a distance she was struck by the difference between the faces of her own children and that of the guy, not in terms of looks or of age, but of intelligence. Was this maternal bias? She looked more closely at Jason and Matthew. They moved with small twitches; they were responsive to subtle stimuli. Their process of building meaning out of the world around them was an active one, sophisticated enough to be quick and invisible. Comparatively this guy's cogs were on full display. He stared into his phone lethargically, his concentration dense rather than assiduous; his whole mien gave the impression that things were overwhelming, that he was being left behind. Extinction loomed. She suddenly felt extremely sorry for him. "Guys like him don't make choices," she said.

"Come again?" Rather than eating more of his body food Mike had decided it was time to clear the meal away; he was busy scraping the leftovers off himself and into the sand.

"People feel positively about whatever's been in their life for a while. Even hate and horror can become familiar. Like the pictures on cigarette packets: the sliced-up lungs, blackened stomas: after a short period of adjustment smokers just associate the images with the good feeling of owning cigarettes. Same thing with a bad relationship.

They go, 'Yes this is bad, but it's what I know, and I like what I know because I know it. You know what I don't like?'"

"What's that?"

"What I *don't* know. Look at this guy. He's scared. He's losing the only thing he knows and he has no way to deal with it or understand it." He was still staring at his phone, squinting in the bright light, moving a few paces every now and then in the shallow water, then stopping to squint harder.

"I think I'm gonna swim," Mike said. "I need cleansing. Boredom's gone, though. It's freaky what an antidepressant other people's misery is."

Eleanor watched her husband struggle to stand, stumble sideways a little as he found his footing, and then attempt to wipe away the more gelatinous remnants of his meal from the front of his Batman swim shorts. "It'll come off in the water," she said. "And, honey, if you can, could you wade over and stand next to our guy? I want to directly compare you with him. The best way to do that is with the cold and unforgiving truth of distance."

"Is it a straight physical comparison or do I get, you know, demeanour-based judgments as well?"

"You'll get the whole meal."

"I love you," Mike said, then he jogged away to frighten his children and criticise their sandcastle.

***

And Eleanor was right: Olly was scared. More than scared. Since Jack's departure the previous day, a fully-fledged terror had not only incubated but broken free of the lab and flourished. A gulf had opened. What was he meant to do? There had been a sudden initial rush of synaptic fire when the answer arrived reflexively: ask Sophie. She'll know.

The void opened again.

Once the painkillers had started to work and he'd managed a shower, he'd spent an indeterminant period sitting on his wet towel on the edge of the bed attempting to find his memory. His last image had been of her walking away from the bar. Vivid colours: her sarong's blood-orange popping against the green, the sky a washed blue. He could even recall the sound of her flip-flops tacking softly against her heels.

But then nothing.

He'd tried as best he could to allow Jack's version of events to fill the empty space, but it simply wouldn't. Instead it remained fiercely blank, as if the segment of time had been forcibly removed from reality and incinerated.

He wondered where she was. Up the coast. A moped tour… What did that mean?

He looked at his phone.

Don't message her with any bullshit about your feelings.

But surely he could ask where she was and find out if she was okay? He just had to keep it simple. Nice and straightforward. He thought about this for a bit, and the more he did, the more convinced he became that it was absolutely the right thing to do. Because it probably wasn't as bad as the Australian had made out (what was his deal anyway?). He and Sophie had fought before, and it wasn't the first time she'd hit him with something—there'd been coffee mugs, a wine glass. It wasn't even the first chair she'd weaponized. He just had to let the hurricane pass and soon it would be all sunflowers and affection. He would buy her something nice and take her to the kind of restaurant she would want to be photographed in.

He opened his phone and thumbed his missive: 'Hey babe sorry for last night hope ur okay. Where are you atm. I'm at the resort XX.' He hit send and examined the screen, awaiting the initial tick to signal that his words had reached the ether.

Tick.

He waited for the second tick to indicate they'd landed on her phone…

No tick.

Of course, this was nothing to panic about. Her phone might have been off—although that didn't seem probable. More likely she was passing through some signal grey zone, twisting between hills, wending through tropical forest. She'd pop out soon, then the second tick would materialise and she would hear the alert and open her phone and the ticks would go blue to signal she'd got it and she would start typing back to say that she forgave him and that she loved him and that she would be back soon kiss kiss kiss.

The forethought of this eventuality calmed Olly, the fantasy enough to tide him over... Until an alternative scenario started sidling its way into the antechamber of his mind.

Moped tour.

Moped tour. Up the coast.

He imagined her riding on the back of one of those shitty little bikes and hugging her arms around some other guy; she was smiling in leopard-print sunlight, zooming through glades of secret forest, auburn hair rippling beneath her helmet. The moped pulled up in a secluded cove. She took the hand of the rider and moved through a narrow track and came out onto an isolated beach and she smiled up at him—this faceless other man—and got down on her knees in the sand and unzipped his fly and–

He found himself caterwauling in his room.

His head began to throb afresh. He stared back down at his phone. One tick. Only one tick. "Calm down!" he shouted to himself. "Everyfing's fine!" He turned it into a mantra: Everything's fine. Everything's fine. Breathe with it. Live it. Order room service. Take your time. Breathe. And when you feel less like a catastrophe, you can reassess things.

But when his food arrived he found his stomach was too tight to allow it. He kept staring at his phone, urging the second tick. He paced the room, turning from wall to wall in wretched hysteria, back and forth and back and forth until he ripped open the room's cupboard, feverishly convinced that he'd find her hiding inside, coiled tight and smiling up at him like the whole thing had been a game. Instead, he discovered his suitcase. Had Jack dragged it over in the night? Had Sophie shoved everything into it before exiling him to the far end of the compound...? He checked through and it seemed to contain only *his* things, all stuffed in hastily. Her passport and travel documents were gone.

That afternoon, with his cell phone permanently in hand, he tried to retrace his movements. He crossed the resort to his original room and looked in through the window. He no longer had a key. He could see Sophie's suitcase by the wardrobe, a dress on the bed—purple: one of her strapless ones—and a pair of pink heels on the floor beneath it. The bed itself was perfectly made, the duvet flat and free of human impression. Instead of comforting Olly, the sight of the place threw him further into confusion. Her clothing seemed like evidence.

He left the room and went to the beach and hung around the areas where they'd taken photos the day before. Only tourists. He found himself looking at the sand as if he might find imprints of her body or tracks he could follow. He'd begun to sweat badly, and he felt a churning sickness that was only partly related to his hangover.

Toward dusk, and still with only one tick on his message, he wondered if he should venture beyond the resort, whether he should find 'The Strip' Jack had mentioned. Nothing had jogged his mind—the amnesia retained a total hold. But it didn't make sense to him that in an inebriated state he'd been able to navigate beyond the hotel. He'd arrived in the dark and knew nothing of the area. What were the chances he'd managed to wander directly into a foreign red-light district?

He was also struggling with time, unable to keep his mind on anything beyond the searing urgency of his absent girlfriend. Throughout the afternoon he'd found himself drifting away into highly concentrated thoughts in which memory and fiction conflated. One moment he was thinking about her face, seen from side-on in the half-light of a bedroom, the next that same bedroom had become a table beside the ocean and the light on her face was the cavorting remainder of the moon reflected off the water; and then she might run from him, and he'd have to chase her, but she would evaporate or slide out of sight or duck sleekly into a crack in the universe and he would realise that he'd been sitting in the same spot on the beach for an hour, or that he'd walked all the way into The Strip without realising it—without noticing that urban life had grown up around him like a ramshackle fungus and that the coastal road had become a hub of traffic and people—a row of bars and night clubs, low-rent backpacker accommodation, neon signs cutting through golden-hour gloaming. How long had it taken him to get there? The place was thriving, a hot steam of life and food. He could hear British voices in the throng, antipodeans, snags of French. It seemed completely impossible for him to have been somewhere this vibrant and yet to have no memory of it, his personal film exposed to harsh sunlight and destroyed.

He crossed the main drag and climbed the front stairs to a bar with a large porch that looked out over the water. He ordered a beer and sat watching the view of the street, the palms and the ocean, and tried not to listen to the conversations of other Westerners. Instead he tuned himself into the song playing through the open doors—Kylie Minogue's *Come Into My World*. He lost his sense of time again. It wasn't Kylie singing, it was Sophie, shimmering, seductive, and she *did* need his love, and he *did* want to come in to her world, and by the time his beer arrived he was on the verge of crying again.

"Everyfing's fine."—Speak the mantra. "Everyfing's *fuckin* fine!"

He checked his phone, but instead of diving straight for WhatsApp, he opened Facebook. Distraction, he thought. Self-preservation. Find something to drag your mind from the furrows of pain. But he couldn't escape her. As soon as the blue and white backdrop resolved, there she was, right at the top of his feed with a crisp new post. He recognised the photo immediately—it was from the beach the day before. He'd taken it. She was posed, looking off into the distance, leaning back and cross-legged and hot and tanned, the ocean a barbiturate of peace-and-love sexuality lying coolly behind her. It was a great picture.

Faggot, he thought.

Fuck.

He read the post: '*Having such a great time in Thailand.*

So lucky to have opportunities to see the world. The people here have such beautiful souls and the cultures are amazing. I'm such a lucky girl. I love all of you and stay perfect XX #girlpower#blessed'

Bitch.

That was his first instinct. Then he was jealous. Then he was angry. Then he loved her intensely, which made him feel horrifically sad. And all of this happened inside the five seconds it took him to read her post, reread it, then stare again at the picture—too quickly for him to parse or digest or come to terms with it. He wanted to crush his phone in his hand. He wanted to leap the fence, drop to the street and run into the sea to drown. He wanted to hold her and cry.

"Mr! Mr! You like ping pong!"

Some gimp beneath him on the pavement. Thai. A tattooed neck and no front teeth. "Wat?"

"Ping pong pussy! Sexy girls. You come see!"

"Not interested, mate."

The guy persisted. "First rate girls. Pussy balloon. Big tick. Two thumbs."

Tick. He went straight back to his phone. She couldn't have posted without some kind of connection. And there it fucking was!—the *second tick*. His message had hit her cell. They hadn't gone blue, but that didn't mean she hadn't read it. She would have been notified. And his message had been short, so the preview would have let her see all of it. She just didn't want to let him know that she'd opened it.

Bitch.

His face was getting hot, and his mind was suddenly awash with graphically depicted scenes of cuckoldry, with glistening flesh and pornographic laughter in which he was the joke. She was mocking him!

Cunt.

He needed to send another message. Now. Right now. Before the sting chilled and he'd thought himself out of it. He'd started to tremble.

"Too gay, Mr? Too gay. You big guy. You like girls—ping pong pussy pop! You come!"

"Fuck off!" Olly barked. The Thai sex-peddler backed away with his hands in the air. Other drinking Westerners pointed or snickered. And now Billy Ocean was playing.

He started writing, allowing predictive to take care of his literacy gaps: *'I know you got my message where are you? I need to know you're okay I deserve to know X'*

He hit send.

One tick. Two ticks. Sophie is online.

"Open the fucken message!" he shouted, indifferent to the stares.

Love really hurts without you! cried the speakers.

But the two little digital ticks remained obstinately grey, tiny angular scratches of her apathy—indicators of a better time and a better life being had elsewhere. "Fuck! Bitch!"

"Hey, bro!" An American voice. "You wanna cool it?"

Olly turned to see a table of hipster backpackers staring at him—college kids who looked collectively like a group that would never have spoken to him if given the choice. Rather than answer, he got up and went, walking toward the resort, the luminescence of The Strip fading behind him, the digital amphetamine of his phone's screen front and centre of his vision. On his left the sun had plunged hard and atomic into the sea; it left an elemental burn that sizzled the horizon and screamed fire into the night. He didn't notice.

He went straight to the front desk and asked for Jack. "The Aussie lad—'e workin tonight?"

The receptionist was a woman. Indian maybe. "I'm sorry," she said. "He's not on. Is there anything I may be able to help you with?"

Olly thought for a moment. He looked back at the receptionist. She was smiling at him in a professional but friendly manner, and it made him want to ask if he could hold her hand while she told him that everything was okay, that everything was fine. "Na," he said. "Fanks."

He wandered the grounds of the resort. Meals were being served by torchlight beneath the palms; waiters drifted like moths; children were releasing sky lanterns at the water's edge. Olly moved through it like a man trapped outside reality, a colourless wraith wedged between dimensions.

Sophie's room remained dark and empty. But he had to watch it, because what else was there to do? He sat burning his retina on her feed, his back against a palm as he maintained a vigil over the entrance—if she came back, she would have to see him. There was no way around it.

He'd *liked* her post—it would've seemed weird for him not to. He'd commented underneath: *lookin good babe* X. And near midnight he messaged her again: short this time, plaintive—just a question mark.

Blue ticks!

Sophie is typing…

A vitriolic openhanded slap: *'Go to sleep fuckstick. I'm alive.'*

The warmth of contact drowned him in exhilarated relief. He found himself slouching onto his back in the grass and breathing heavily—it was like coming up on ecstasy, like finishing a race; he felt bathed, breathless, drilled into the earth. He could smell the sea again and feel the breeze and hear the edges of the night. But he didn't want to blow it—things were fragile. He responded to the message simply and unequivocally, just an X, then he returned to his room and masturbated himself unconscious.

INT. EXECUTIVE OFFICE – DAY

The executive shifts in his chair. "You sure you want to show him masturbating? Is that really essential to the narrative?"

The filmmaker answers without even pausing for thought. "First off, we're talking *implied* rather than *shown*—you know, a shot of his face in the demented contortion of autoerotica, caught in the blue light of the moon through venetian blinds. But either way, yes, it's totally essential to an explication of the narrative's themes. The noir shadow-slats across his face will signal he's a prisoner of his sex instinct, that he's a kind of zoo animal. And that's all part of the story. And frankly it's important if we want an even vaguely honest characterisation of the modern male."

"Okay, okay," the exec says, holding up his palms. "Just checking. Keep the wanking."

EXT. BEACH FRONT – LATE MORNING

While the pre-bed communication had allowed him to sleep, it did nothing to settle him in the new day. Within a second of leaving the dreamscape Olly recalled that he was alone, remembered that he didn't know where Sophie was, and felt with frosty certainty that she was never coming back.

His instability was exacerbated by proximity to her images. Although he ate his breakfast at an outdoor table overlooking the beach, he didn't see it. Instead he trawled her social media, adrift in anti-paginated image streams of his girlfriend: Sophie looking coy in a South London park; Sophie dripping wet and looking seductively to the right; Sophie on Westminster Bridge in heels and a short dress, half turned as she floated a smile across the Thames. With his eyes on his phone, it was like she hadn't left at all, like they weren't physically apart. If he looked away, he had to face the alternative.

By late morning he was standing calf-deep in the water and squinting at his screen, flicking back and forth between pictures and WhatsApp, maintaining vigilance. He had to know when she was online. He'd messaged her again at breakfast: *'eatin and chillin. when you back? X'*. He'd even sent a photo of himself with his fruit bowl and flat white, an awkward selfie with a fraudulent smile. But he felt it was important. He had to prove to her that he was alive and functional and not cutting his wrists. He had to be worth coming back to.

One tick.

Where was she now? The swirl had started all over again and he was trying to keep it together. He held his phone up to the sky as he waded, reaching into the firmament in the hope of catapulting his message. It wasn't working. He returned to the comfort of her images: Sophie looking dreamy in the latticed morning light from a window; Sophie in her lingerie with her back against a doorframe; Sophie tanning in the park.

He didn't even notice the guy standing next to him in the water until he'd started talking.

"Wha?" Olly said, annoyed that he had had to look up.

"Are you getting any good reception out here?" Mike repeated.

"Yeah," Olly said. His head went straight back to the phone. The last thing he wanted was a conversation with some American lurker.

"You know, if you hold the phone to your head, your skull works as a natural amplifying device. It makes sending and receiving messages easier." Olly glanced at the guy again, his interest in the information having been rapidly piqued. "Like this," Mike continued, lifting his hand to a spot above his ear. "Just press the top of the phone here and the data signal catches more effectively."

"Foreal?"

"Yup. For *absolutely* real."

Olly tentatively moved the phone up and nudged it against the side of his head. "Like this?"

"Nearly. Turn it on an angle so it's just the top corner touching. And a little higher up the skull."

"Like this?"

"Perfect."

"Fanks, mate." Olly turned his back on the American and continued with his shallow wade along the shore, now more confidant he wouldn't miss anything.

"You're a bastard," Eleanor said as Mike approached.

He'd been reluctant to turn around, lest he raise the guy's suspicions. "He still doing it?"

"Of course he's still doing it."

Mike sank back into his sun lounger and watched. The guy was moving with more volition now—hoping, it appeared, to combine momentum and his new method of signal augmentation to maximise its efficacy. "How'd I look next to him?"

"Short and a bit fat, but I have to say you had

noticeably more *joie de vivre*."

"And that counts for a lot, right?"

"It counts for something."

The couple watched on. Eleanor ordered more champagne; Mike ordered prawns. Jason and Matthew played in the sand.

INT. EXECUTIVE OFFICE – DAY

The executive gets up and looks out the window; from this, the third floor, he can see across the city. At the moment it is a clear day, except for a haze that seems to linger in the south—pollution from the highways and factories. The filmmaker has paused in his explanation and is grateful for it; his hands have been working overtime in the creation of shapes and images. He feels he is not only a filmmaker but a magician, a prestidigitator whose true skill lies in conjuring worlds through the interplay of voice and gesture.

"How much sympathy are we supposed to have for this guy?" asks the exec. He does not turn from the window. "For Olly, I mean. Is the viewer meant to like him? Are we meant to be enjoying his pain?"

"Everyone's a little bit of a sadist," says the

filmmaker. "And we don't often admit it but most of us like seeing bad things happen to good looking people. The killer's really the hero in a slasher film. Depends on the individual, though. We all see the world differently. Spectatorship 101."

The exec turns from the window: "You didn't really answer the question there, Max."

"Well, how much sympathy do *you* have for him?"

"I think that's my issue: not as much as I should have. But is that because I'm callous and jaded, or because this guy is, in fact, universally pathetic? I mean, outside his pectorals and his youth, he doesn't have a lot going for him. He's stupid, he's fixated on someone awful, and he lacks basic people skills. And as soon as he gets an indication that she's okay, he calls her a bitch and a cunt."

The filmmaker lets this assessment hang between them for a moment before responding. "That sounds like a normal male to me."

"We don't want to make him more, I don't know..." The exec pretends to search for a word even though he already has the one he wants lined up. "Dignified? It would make him a hell of a lot more likeable."

The filmmaker remains unruffled. "I'm going to need you to trust me on this one. We're characterising here so we can create foils in the scenes to come—and you and I both know it's all about foils. It's vital: he needs to be undignified; he needs to wallow in emotional ignominy; he needs to be pathetic. His behaviour reflects what we tend to hate most about ourselves. I want him to mirror male failings to the point that the viewer is repelled enough to laugh at him."

"I see."

"He needs to be emasculated and humiliated." The filmmaker says this with sharp intensity. He uses his hand as a blade, cutting through the air as he speaks. "He's symbolic: a manifestation of hilarious castration. His dick needs to be sliced off and carried away by a bird."

INT. RESORT FRONT DESK – AFTERNOON

It was shortly after Jack began his afternoon reception shift that Olly materialised looking harried and very much on edge. At the time, the Australian was checking in a family—smiling courteously and speaking with the internationally recognised soft tones of professional hospitality—so Olly waited, frantically pacing back and forth near the entrance, pressing the corner of his phone to his head, then looking at it, then repeating the process. He didn't seem to notice that he was the cause of the automatic doors opening and closing in spasms, nor did he seem to register the digital bell he was triggering every time they did, and Jack had to break off his conversation with the new guests and ask him politely to either take a seat or wait outside. Olly chose the seat and returned to his mystifying phone-to-skull practice.

"Mate," Jack said, once a porter had shuffled the

Sandersons and their luggage out of the foyer. "The fuck are you doing?"

Olly leapt up and raced to the desk. Between the muscles, the six-plus frame and gleam of madness, Jack had to fight the urge to grab a makeshift weapon among the stationery. "As she come back!?" His eyes seemed to wobble in their sockets. "Ya know where she is!?"

"Easy, sunshine. Everything okay?"

"Na! She aint back! I fought ya said she'd be back!"

Jack looked nervously around the reception area. A coach was pulling up outside, and he was aware a distraught lout was not the best first impression for arriving guests. "Look, I need you to take a breath for me, matey-moo. Can ya do that?" Olly seemed to twitch a little, then nodded. "So she's not back from the moped tour?"

"Na. I mean yeah." He shook his head like a child, shuffling his thoughts into a workable order. "I mean, she asnt come back."

"And I bet you messaged her even though I told you not to, right?"

"I jus needed ta know she was awight…"

Through the front window Jack watched as a stream of retirees descended from the coach, a swathe of pastels and hula shirts. "Listen to me carefully: I want you to go hit the bar and have a beer, or go for a swim, try to chill out a bit. I finish at eight. I'll come meet you then and I'll have information about tour return times. Everything you need, okay. I'm sure she's fine. Stay calm. She'll be back tonight, I'm certain."

The automatic doors opened and the wave of new guests began babbling their way inside. Olly didn't seem to notice. "Did ya pack me bag?" The question came out as a demand.

"What?"

"When ya moved me ta the cabin? Did ya pack me bag?"

"Some of it, yeah." Jack was looking into the mob of geriatric arrivals—white hair, fat moustaches, walking sticks. "Look, mate, I'll see you later—eight o'clock, at The Warbler."

"The wat?"

"The bar, mate." Jack winked in a way he hoped conveyed camaraderie before turning his attention to the crowd forming behind Olly. "This must be the Steinholtz Party," he smiled. "My name is Jack. May I welcome you to–"

Olly found himself being pushed away like tidal silt. Suddenly he was outside again, this time by the fountain at the entrance of the resort. He pressed his cell phone back against his head.

When his migraine began that afternoon, thudding dully at first, then swelling into a bright point of light, he capitulated to Jack's suggestion, ditched his mobile, and went for a proper swim.

He paddled out until it was too deep to stand and let himself float, trying, in some way, to let his problems drift off. It was becoming clear to him that he was not a man comfortable with being alone. His thoughts didn't have the shape or structure to support long periods of uninterrupted thinking; nor was his mind blank enough to find Zen, and although not fully conscious of it, it was for this reason he preferred company—his mates at the pub, Sophie, even the sound of the TV; other people lent him an internal scaffolding and made things easier. Around jokes concerning his manhood and conversation about darts, he had a net to fall into; if his girlfriend was telling him what to do and how to feel, his processing apparatus continued to operate. But in times of solitude…? It was remarkable how quickly he broke down, becoming confused and despondent, paralysed by basic choices, unable to sort what was relevant and what was detritus.

But today—in the sedative of the water, at least—he was different. He lay back and looked at the sky and wiggled his arms and legs to keep himself afloat. With his ears beneath the surface he could hear the blood pulsing in his head, his own heartbeat—which was startlingly fast— and he could feel the cocoon of the water itself. He was far enough out to be alone, and for the first time not just since the start of the trip but possibly for years, he tried to gain some control over the fidgeting wreckage that constituted his mind: be calm, he thought. He focused solely on that notion, untensing his body, loosening his spine. And then, remarkably, it started to happen. He felt everything slowly unwind and unfurl—his biceps felt rubbed down, his calf muscles kneaded into softness. He tried to become the surface of the water, for on this breezeless afternoon it retained the quality of a pond; he too was this stillness. Soon he no longer had to kick or paddle; he'd gained a composure that let him drift without expending effort, without sinking, and in this state he found his eyes half closing into a glaze, the warm light of the sky pressing against the skin of his eyelids, leaning on the capillaries; his vision became a yawning orange, and within this nascent serenity he found images and sounds that settled him—rain sliding down a window, rain on a roof, feet crunching through snow, a lawnmower two streets over on a summer's day. A glade on a country lane... He lived in this state, and it felt for a moment as if the universe itself were rubbing gentle circles on his temples—a divine touch that willed his headache beyond his flesh and out into the world where it could be separated and dissolved in the expanse of everything. His heart had slowed right down, and when he finally opened his eyes and registered the sense of reality again—the people on the sand, the dampened sounds of beach music and boat engines—he felt much better. Whole. Stable.

He swam back to the shore in a lackadaisical way, pleased with himself, feeling as if he were in control and in command. The water parted for him because it *was* him—they were one and the same. All he had to do was hold this feeling and nothing would touch him.

He walked coolly up the beach, dried himself off and checked his phone. A message from Sophie: *'Stop contacting me fuckdick. I don't want to see you. We're thru.'*

INT. EXECUTIVE OFFICE – DAY

"Good," says the executive. "I like that certainty. Neat tonal antithesis as well: tranquillity followed by savagery. That's nice. That's important."

"I think so, too." The filmmaker presses on, drawing lines in the air to illustrate the relationship between sound and image. "So we get an audio-bridge. The jazz bleeds in, and we fade into the darkness of The Warbler—a genuine noir shot. It pulls out of the sky, past the handcrafted sign—lit in amber yellow—then down into a close-up of Jack's face. Expression is crucial here: he should have a look which mixes embarrassment with the pure annoyance of having to do something tedious. A look that suggests he's contractually obliged to complete a task that he finds disgusting. Does that look have a name? Cantankerous acquiescence? I don't know. And we can hear a choked masculine sobbing…"

EXT. THE WARBLER – NIGHT

"Look, mate, don't cry. Shit." Jack's eyes nipped across the locale. They weren't the only people drinking at The Warbler—the place was dotted with guests enjoying flambeaux lighting and wine and a gentle sea breeze. He'd already moved Olly to the darkest corner, out on the fringes of the night shadow where the speakers were playing prefabricated mood jazz. He'd hoped this would be discreet enough, but now he was considering moving him out onto the beach.

In the aftermath of Sophie's detonation, Olly had rapidly typed a blizzard of messages, most of which were garbled and indecipherable, his brain not connecting with his fingers and compounding his deficiencies as a writer. But it didn't matter whether they were shambolic word fragments, sonnets or Linear B—like everything else he'd sent, they'd jammed in the purgatory of a single tick and left him stalled in his voiceless nightmare. But then it got worse, because having received the message, he'd then moved as if by rote to their original room and pressed his hands against the glass and looked inside. It was a sudden evisceration. Her things were gone. No suitcase, no dress on the bed, no high-heel shoes. The place looked like they'd never inhabited it.

He'd missed her.

She'd come and gone and had made no effort to find him.

Now he was crying in the corner of a bar named The Warbler, six beers deep, and hoping a man he didn't really know might comfort him in some way.

"Look, mate," Jack said, still peering around the place. "I'm all for indulging in the feels, but you've gotta hold it together a bit. We're in public. I work here. Man-up for a moment."

Olly's chest heaved as he tried to restrain himself. "Yeah," he said.

"It's okay—you'll have plenty of time for a weep-a-thon when you're alone and ignoring my advice again. You still got my wank-hanky—the one I gave you?"

"Huh?"

"Here." Jack forcibly handed him a napkin. "Wipe your face and drink your beer." He watched him press the material to his face and blow his nose.

Olly looked up from his hands, his lost eyes a

lachrymose quiver in the torchlight: "Sall appenen so fast…"

"Look, matey-moo. I'm not going to lie to you and say everything's tip-top, because nothing ever is—it's a swirl of chaos and rot and everyone's alone. But, mate, frankly no one cares about your suffering. It's *shit* suffering. In the scheme of things, I mean. Get some perspective. Remember, a decade ago all this was rubble—totally washed away. Hundreds of thousands dead."

Olly looked around, searching it seemed for evidence of destruction, unsure if the Australian was taking the piss. "Sa joke innit? Aint been no war ere."

Jack took a breath and squinted, then released the breath like a car tyre losing air. He looked out toward the darkness of the ocean. "Seriously, Olly? Boxing Day, 2004?"

"Wat? So?"

"This your first time out of England, Olly?"

"Nah," he said. "Wenna Scotland wiff me school. Wanned ta go wiff Soph. And ta France." He looked back at his hands, then at his phone—one tick—then at his beer. He seemed to be on the verge of crying again.

Jack stared hard at Olly for a moment in a way that an outside observer would have struggled to decipher. Pity? Contempt? Some other oblique sentiment…? "I'm gonna tell you a story about a lemur," he said at last. "You know what a lemur is?"

"Naw."

"Small. Furry. Four legs. Fuck it. A koala. You know

what a koala looks like?"

"Yeah. Like a teddy bear innit?"

Jack took a sip of his drink and placed it back on the table between them. "So I want you to imagine this: there's this koala and he has a balloon. You with me?"

"Yeah."

"Now, he loves this balloon. But one day, when he's tying his koala shoes, he looks over and realizes his balloon's gone. It's floated away. How does he feel?"

"…Sad?"

"Yes he does! He feels sad. He feels sad because he's lost his balloon—that's just natural."

"Yeah, yeah."

"In the meantime the balloon floats off, and maybe someone else finds it and enjoys it, or maybe it just slowly loses air and gets all wrinkled and depressed, or maybe it just outright pops—which is the hope. But whatever happens, it's just a balloon. The koala, on the other hand, is a koala. Do koala's need balloons to be happy, Olly?"

"Sa good question innit."

"Not really. Point is, the koala should just say fuck the balloon, right…?" Jack watched the man process this dilemma slowly. "If you're struggling with the symbols, Sophie's the balloon in this story. I thought that was clear…"

"But I *love* er, mate. Ya don't get it."

The urge to punch Olly in the face came on hot and fast. "Look, you *don't* love her. Nothing about the noxious horror that was your relationship was anywhere near love."

Jack collected himself for a moment, seeking clarity. Once again he found himself breathing out slowly. "Here's the thing, she's not really like a balloon. She's more like bird shit. She's more like one of those little dinosaurs that spat paralysing agent into the face of its prey before devouring it—and koalas don't need those either. She's feasting on your spinal cord, fella."

"She aint like that…" Olly said. He was suddenly resolute about this point. "Ya don't know her."

But Jack did know her. And he knew exactly what she was like and exactly how bad she was. He had proof, too, and it was becoming obvious to him that he would need to show this guy. Unless the napalm was deployed, there would be no forward movement. Men, women and children would have to melt in the fire from the sky; babies needed to burn. *We had to destroy the village in order to save it.* He got out his phone. "Come down to the beach with me," he said.

"Why?"

"We need to pop a balloon. Kill a dinosaur. Whatever. It'll be fun. I promise."

INT. EXECUTIVE OFFICE – DAY

Lunch has arrived. The exec has chosen the dim sum and left the filmmaker with the Thai noodles. Both beer bottles are open on the exec's desk. "Some of this seems quite deeply rooted in your life," says the exec. "I mean, in terms of the ferocity of feeling."

"You sound like my high school guidance counsellor. It's a bromide, sure, but I resolve my issues in my art. I like dealing with stuff through my characters."

Having already struggled, the exec is considering giving up on his chopsticks and using his fingers; he lays them to the side for a moment. "And you think everybody should go through that therapy with you? That's not what an audience is paying for."

"Look, all the good directors do it. All the good artists do it. I'm sublimating. And blending. And I'm distilling it all into a film that seeks some truth about human experience."

"You think this Olly character reflects a truth about human experience?" The exec lifts an eyebrow as he says this but does not hold the expression; instead he returns to his dumplings, this time with his fingers.

The filmmaker shrugs.

"Death and sex, my friend," the exec continues, his mouth full. "That's all that really matters to the viewer. Hell, that's all that matters to me."

The filmmaker looks toward the window for a moment and considers whether to say what he's about to say, then goes for it. "I used to download all the beheadings, all the really savage execution videos, and just any creepy 4chan-style viral content where someone was videoed suiciding or accidently frying themselves on a downed powerline or something. Then I'd take a montage of graphic pornography and just overlay the two, so you could see both images at the same time. After a while, it does just start to look like the same dance."

"Jesus, Max. This is what I'm talking about. A therapist should be hearing this, not the guy you're pitching a film to." The exec takes a swig of his beer. "Not that I'm judging. How are the noodles?"

"Excellent," the filmmaker says. "You want to try some?"

The exec waves his hand to signal no. "I don't like to cross-reference my meals." He puts a whole dumpling in his mouth and reaches for a serviette to catch the runnel of soy sauce escaping down his chin.

"That's the thing," the filmmaker says. "I quite like to cross-reference—beyond food, I mean. Overlapping is good. You actually *see* things that way. And why does it make me deviant if I want to examine all aspects of human life—from ninjas to necrophiles, as my mother used to say."

"Your mother didn't used to say that."

"This is the world I live in—and I only get to live in it once, by the way—and I want to see and understand and link as much of it as I can before I'm chock-full of cancer."

"You think you'll be a cancer, do you?" the exec asks.

The filmmaker ignores the question and ploughs ahead. "If anything, I don't think I'm deviant enough. I was shown this Italian painting the other day, from the 1920s. It was of a guy driving a convertible through picturesque countryside. Except, he's standing up to do it. Quite a feat, right? But he needs to be standing up because that's the only way he can have his pants down and his dick in the woman's mouth. I assume she's his girlfriend. And she's semi-naked and on all fours. Her hands are down the passenger's seat, her mid-section arched through the middle of the car, her legs in the footwell of the back seat. And she needs to be like this because it's the only way that the guy's dog can do her at the same time. I think it was a Doberman."

"She's sucking his dick while the dog fucks her?"

"While they're driving along. I assume it's his dog. It

could be her dog…"

"Probably a stretch. I'm not an expert in this stuff but the misogyny doesn't sound sub-textual."

"Semiotic nightmare, right?" The filmmaker smiles. "This really isn't something I'd suggest to your wife, by the way. Go with the ping pong balls first. But my point is, I thought it was a great painting—filthy, full of cross-reference: it's got obscene sex, speed dreams, power struggles, death fascinations. *Bestiality*—used both literally and as metaphor. Imagine if the artist had had access to the internet?"

"How did you find it? Can I google it?" The exec has his phone out. "What do I search?"

"Finish your dim sum first."

EXT. GRANGER UNIVERSITY PARKING LOT – AFTERNOON

Economics 101 wasn't a particularly popular class to teach among the faculty at Ohio's Granger University. It was massive, for one, and it was generally populated with the insipid faces of recent high school graduates, nearly half of whom would drop out before the end of their first year. But Professor Verne Williams always volunteered in cheery fashion. First of all, it was a chance for him to stamp his mark as a lecturer. He felt he had a style that lent gravitas to most subjects. He tended to speak in long, clear sentences and with a measured voice, and he had cultivated the look of the gently eccentric academic: grey hair at the temples, reading glasses that could be used as a prop, a habit of conducting with his right hand as he spoke. He was also beginning to run to fat, which gave him added scholastic appeal. If only it hadn't also triggered a fitness campaign by his wife. "It's *not* an aesthetic issue," she'd said to him. "It's about your health. I'm not put off by your body hair or your persistent perspiration, but I would be if those things threatened to kill you. You're in your forties for Christ's sake, Verne! Look after yourself."

But Williams also took Economics 101 for a reason beyond his reputational vanity. Put simply, he wanted to remain in close intellectual proximity to the ideas in the course, to have them floating around in the active part of his brain rather than the filing system, and the best way to do that, he felt, was to teach it time and time again. To leave knowledge dormant was to do it a disservice; what was the point of the concepts he'd ingested unless he could live with them and work with them and apply them to the reality in which he existed? And of course, these were *important* ideas, foundational. And the lesson he'd taught only an hour earlier was one of the most crucial— the trap lecture: the lecture in which he laid out the concept of Adam Smith's invisible hand.

He wondered now, as he drove through leafy suburban streets in the early afternoon, how many of his students challenged the basic assumption, the premise on which everything rested, that *human beings are rational actors*, and that to act rationally is to act out of self-interest. "Of course," he'd stated to his students (aided with the help of a neat flow chart) "we see this play out in the fundamentals of market competition. By being self-interested we take advantage of each other's greed. If Joe and Andy both sell apples but Joe is charging too much, Andy will undercut him and Joe will fail unless he drops his prices to the appropriate market value. If Susan, a fat-cat bourgeois factory owner, doesn't pay her workers enough, then her workers will leave and work for Anna, who pays better wages. Thus, the invisible hand strokes and guides and lovingly cajoles the market into a sensible order."

How many of them had bothered to think that one through?

How many of them had looked at themselves and the world around them and challenged the initial statement?

Fact: human beings are not rational. And even if they want to behave in a self-interested way, the dynamic clutter of the world usually prevents them from doing so. Workers don't just leave a job if they're not being paid well. Alcoholism gets in the way. Or a sick mother. Or laziness or typhoons or a swollen appendix. Life is a game of chess where the pieces keep moving before you have a chance to move them yourself. Dream chess.

It was all there, Williams thought. And it was always important to embrace the concepts of chaos and complexity. It was vital to constantly acknowledge that they were the most significant factors to consider, that *they* were the dominant forces in of themselves.

He was already rehearsing what he would tell his class at the end of the semester, hoping to catch and hold the young and critically minded. He started orating it in the car as he drove, trialling the language with the bass of his voice: "This density of human motivation, especially when combined with the infinite factors in operation beyond the individual human agent—the global shifts, the plagues and wars; the blowing of the zephyr across wheat fields and the tiny screams of infant lungs—these are relevant to everything and therefore incalculable. Remember, nobody actually knows what the stock market will do, and there is no formula that will predict the random shocks of life. Both the world and the people that inhabit it behave irrationally."

Pause for effect. Let the words settle.

"Rationality itself is a *fallible human construct*, and in the end you will find that it does not apply in economics, or politics, or in your relationships with one another. Hopefully my words will give you comfort during your first divorce."

Williams was still repeating this to himself as he pulled his Hyundai into the driveway of his home. Although he was unsure about finishing on the downbeat divorce comment, the overall gist would be perfect for the end-of-term summary—right before he sent his students into the madness of Christmas. He parked the car and went quickly into the house and straight to the note pad on the kitchen counter. He had to get the sentences down before they slipped from his mind, and in his intellectual fervour he was forced hold up his hand to stop the house cleaner from talking to him while he jotted… Except, now that he'd written it down it had all started to seem pretentious... He turned to the cleaner. "Sorry, Adriana. That was extremely rude of me—I just had to get that out before I lost it to the zeitgeist."

"Okay," she said. Her vowels were wide and over pronounced. It annoyed Williams that his cleaner was from Honduras. Her existence in what was nominally a servant's role made him feel like a racist.

"Money's on the table," he said, smiling and trying to eradicate the itchy notion that he was an instrument of oppression. She nodded and moved to collect the envelope. "Same time next week?"

"*Si.*"

And then she was gone and the Professor's afternoon opened up. His daughter would be out till late; his wife was going straight from work to a book club dinner.

So that he might clear his head of the day's thinking and appease his spouse's wish that he live longer, he committed to a jog around the local park. He changed clothes. He paid lip service to the concept of stretching. Then he was out the door. Of course, between his weight and general lack of coordination, the experience was a nightmare. Despite never getting much above a walk, he soaked his shirt through, and while out of breath and struggling he was tormented by what a younger version of himself might have made of the spectacle—a twenty-year-old Verne Williams sitting at one of the tables near the pond, watching on and vowing never to become the waddling, hairy disaster that was dragging itself along the path and looking for a spot to die. "Don't look so disgusted," he wheezed at his imaginary self: "This is where you're heading and there's nothing you can do!" He briefly envisaged his own carcass being fed on by vultures, a crumpled sack of running clothes and rotting fat.

Back at the house he took off his shoes and his shirt and towelled himself down to prevent his sweat from soaking the upholstery, then he sat heavily on the couch and stared into nothing for a few minutes while his body recalibrated. When the hum in his ears faded, he opened the laptop on the coffee table in front of him, and flush with post-exercise endorphins and a mind empty of the day's challenges, he logged on. He'd timed everything perfectly.

What Professor Williams tuned into next was not something he had arrived at by accident. It was the end result of a long process of self-discovery, active searching, and experimentation. For who, as an adolescent, truly understands themselves enough to know implicitly what turns them on? In the end, it's a delicate interplay between experienced reality, memory, and the coloured pastiche of fantasy, and more often than not a person's most acute and effective erotic fantasy is simply an admixture of past experiences, current cultural contexts, and preëxisting prejudices: let's all dare to suck dick in a dorm room; time to fuck your stepdaughter!; there's a champagne gangbang in the VIP lounge—foam up your cocks!!!!! So it goes with the lusty hopes and wet dreams of the common suburban denominator. But for a discerning man like Professor Williams, the standard co-ed slut party wasn't going to cut it. It might have once—in the age before the industrialization of sex and when he too was a gawky freshman without a gut—but not anymore. Now he needed something more bespoke. Something that existed beyond the categories and acronyms of the mass consumption fuck sites; no more DP, CFNM, BBW; no more threesomes, fivesomes or POV anal creampie specials. Sexually speaking, that stuff was plebeian fast food—a digital McDonalds of pornography, its floors slippery with the semen of the unwashed and unrefined. He was done with it. That's not to say he knew what he was looking for, though—just that Big Macs and Lube Sauce no longer did it for him (*Fuck my housekeeper? But she's just finished cleaning!*).

But where to turn to next? Too sensitive for simulated rape and domination sites, too European for animated tentacles. Too sane for the furry brigade and too queasy for the men who fuck goats, or dogs, or donkeys. And for a while he had felt lost, like he'd caught the wrong bus to the weird part of town; like he'd wandered into someone else's party knowing he didn't belong but then stayed for a while anyway to eat some of the free food and watch guy-on-guy anal tonguing… The sense of confusion and displacement had begun to affect his real life, leaking in through the gaps in his personal cladding; his lecturing suffered; he was short with his wife and daughter. A piece of Maslow's pyramid was missing and his whole world seemed to be on a kind of lurch.

Then he happened to read the bio of a webcam

channel listed as DaisyFuckYou:

My boyfriend is a fucking joke. Let the bidding begin if you want to see some hot pain.

The profile pic featured a trashy but conventionally attractive woman and a guy wearing aviator sunglasses. They looked like a pair of contestant hopefuls who'd failed in the selection round of a reality show Verne would never have watched anyway, so he held scant hope they would save him from his masturbatory malaise. And he'd been in stranger places, of course: he'd seen *The Horror!* at the end of the river; DaisyFuckYou would mean nothing to him—just another flesh show, another disappointment in the bleary tedium of modern erotica.

How wrong he was.

And who would have guessed he could ever have found the gutter-sludge mix of Daisy's objectively disgusting voice and her outright verbal bile attractive? With the sound off, she was meaningless—more painted steak in life's grotesque butchery. But when the deformed cadences and caustic vocabulary returned, it pulled Verne into a private frenzy. She wasn't even talking dirty. She was simply talking *mean*, sitting there in her bra and knickers and calling her audience faggots and cunts. It took him a little while to figure out what it was she was actually saying, to first decipher the code of her language and then come to grips with the narrative thread of her channel. Then he cottoned on: not only was she selling the live feed of sexual congress with her boyfriend and doing it *without his apparent knowledge or consent*, she was laying down prices for specific acts of violence she was prepared to inflict on him—acts ranging from the tame to, well... How much were people willing to pay? How much was Verne willing to pay?

That afternoon, when the feed came online and DaisyFuckYou was live, Verne was all paid up. $US200 seemed steep, and he'd had to transfer in advance with no guarantee she'd come through, but she'd never failed him before, and given his level of psycho-sexual gratification he was more than willing to trust her. He was a happy customer—one of many who frequented the stream, coming for the sex and staying for the senseless violence and humiliation.

He slipped off his underpants and let his weight rest back into the sofa. Sure enough, there was her boyfriend (the guy was never given a name) climbing onto the bed and lying on his back with his signature sunglasses—a patient, really; a subject. Maybe even an effigy. And there was our girl, climbing right on top with zero foreplay, then shimmying, writhing, and working for her money through a good fifteen minutes of invective-laden theatrics. But this was only the entrée, and Professor Williams had never been big on perfunctory soups or token salmon. He wanted the main course. "Do it," he said to the screen. But he didn't need to say anything. All the signs were there. It was about to happen: her words had jumbled and broken and become a dogged, elongated growl, growing in intensity and power, pulling louder and harder. It was as if the sound itself were some fevered demon trying to climb up and out of her throat and explode in a rain of blood from the ceiling. And then it was a scream—full-bodied and torrential—until her words finally broke free of the tortured syllable: "Ya dumb fucken faggit!" She punched him in the face as hard as she could.

On the other side of the globe Professor Williams cheered as if he were watching a football match, half rising from the sofa, shooting his fist into the air and shouting "*Yeeeesss! Take that you fucking pretty boy!*" His turgid member pointed happily into the otherwise tranquil atmosphere of his family's living room, his large naked body quivering with satisfaction in the soft afternoon light.

INT. EXECUTIVE OFFICE – DAY

The filmmaker isn't saying anything. He seems distracted by internal thoughts. The executive is spinning very slowly in his chair, his gaze tilted slightly upward. Lunch is finished.

EXT. BEACH FRONT – MID-AFTERNOON

When the Murphy family set up on the beach for another day of gorging and alcohol, Olly was the first thing they noticed. He was squatting near the water's edge like a burnt-out gargoyle, his face pointed at the sand, his forearms resting on his knees while his hands dangled absently in space. Although they ignored him initially, his lack of movement as the hours passed made this more difficult. The tide came in and started washing at his feet. His shadow gradually changed shape and position.

"Guy's like a sundial," Mike said, adjusting himself back into a recliner after a short but emphysemic session chasing his kids. Over the course of only a week he'd managed to put on an abrupt and unhealthy amount of weight, and he felt it now as an emerging blubber suffocating his organs while he tried to get comfortable. "Think his phone ran out of battery?"

"Looks like he's the one out of battery," Eleanor said, lowering her paperback. "Should we tell someone...?" She turned to her husband. "Doesn't that look like a psychotic episode to you? I mean, he's catatonic."

Mike was still struggling to find an appropriate lounging posture, wriggling and shifting. "I don't think this thing's working properly."

"What, the recliner? It's fine. Sit still."

"Maybe I've had too much coffee. And I feel gassy. Do you feel gassy?"

"I don't feel gassy," Eleanor said.

"Why don't you feel gassy?"

"Please stop saying gassy, Michael."

"Flatulent? Bloated? A methane zeppelin of tissue and fat? Imagine a sky filled with human zeppelins, stretched and puffed out, like parade balloons, except they have real live human faces on them that turn slowly and stare at you from above, and every now and then one catches fire and explodes and drifts down slowly, an inferno of body parts smelling of BBQ meat—and there's always someone on hand to shout, '*Oh, the humanity!*'" He'd stopped wriggling.

"You finished?"

"What's wrong? You usually love horror hypotheticals."

"It's that guy. He's bumming me out."

Mike considered Olly again, the unnatural stillness. "Just think of him as a totem pole or something. Or like a reminder of how great it is not to be him." Eleanor started to smile. He continued: "See? If you think of it that way then he's like a spiritual symbol. All hail the Squatting Sad Man."

"But seriously, look at him. Something's broken."

"So? Look, I don't want to sound like an ass here, but a lot of people are broken. Everywhere. You weren't concerned about the beggars on the street when we went into town yesterday; how is this dipshit any different?"

Eleanor put her book down completely and sat up. "You're right, that does make you sound like an ass."

Mike shrugged. "It's what I do. Besides, we go on holiday to take a break from the pain and misery in the real world. This is your week of *not being a social worker*. Honestly, it's bad form for him to be clouding the resort with his negativity—*that's* what you should be telling someone about. We're here so we can have our own idle time. We're not here to deal with this chump's maladjusted psyche."

Eleanor reached out and rested her hand affectionately on Mike's stomach. "You make an excellent series of points, dear husband. However, you must remember that we've being getting free shit by the truckload because of his misery, so I feel we owe it to the guy to tell a staff member about his mental collapse. Maybe we should give thanks to the Squatting Sad Man for all he's done for us…"

It made sense. Mike sighed and stood up—with just a little difficulty—and stretched as if he had awoken from a long and peaceful slumber. "Boys!" he called out. His sons were busy flicking wet sand at each other on the foreshore. "Come up here a minute would you."

Of course, the Murphys couldn't have known the sordid truth behind Olly's personal nightmare, the peculiarly repugnant stitching of his pain, but it's difficult to divine how they would have felt about it had they been told. Would they have expressed sympathy for the torment the guy was going through, or would they have pointed their fingers and laughed? Jack had opted for the latter approach the previous night as he'd stood with Olly on the shore and played a video he had on his phone—one in which Olly was lying on his back in his girlfriend's British bedroom while she rode him and swore at him and slapped him repeatedly in the face. The phone's screen had stood out with supernatural clarity in the darkness, its luminescence scratching at his eyeballs, her voice jabbing into the night air in small treble thrusts, as if it were trying to pierce something. "Fucken fuck ya!" she said on the little display. "Ya fuckeny cuntscrape innit!"

"You see, mate…" Jack said after Olly had failed to respond to the news in any noticeable way, the full scope of the betrayal having been laid out for him in easy-to-understand sentences. "If you adjust your perspective on this, it's actually pretty funny. I mean, it's not funny as in permissible. In fact, I think what she's done here is actually illegal and would probably grab her some jail time if she weren't a hot chick and you didn't come across as such a wombat, but it's certainly not worth killing a lot of people over... Mate? Is that what you're thinking of doing? Killing people?"

The screen was off and the phone was away now, but Olly could still see it: the glowing rectangle against the backdrop, the saturated colours: it had been branded on his episodic memory in a process so violent that it had leaked and fried parts of his cerebral cortex as well, and when Jack took his arm and shook it, it was like the brain meat was still cooking. This was Olly's Fallujah. His personal Jonestown. An internalised massacre all his own. Jack shook his arm again, and this time the Englishman seemed to register, shaking it off with a violence and personal assertion that was out of character. "Fuck off!" he snapped. He moved in circles in the darkness, his face crunched and lined.

"You know, people associate moods with places. It's not just that whenever you come to Thailand from now on you'll feel bad, it's that every time you feel bad, you'll think of Thailand. Weird, huh."

"Fuckin aint true!" Olly shouted. "Ya makin it up!"

"Jesus, mate. First of all, keep your fucking voice down. I know we're on a beach, but this is a resort and people have paid to have a good time. Have a little respect. Second, why would I make this up? Do you wanna look at the actual channel and see what she says about you?"

"Show me the channel!" His voice boomed into the

darkness.

"Mate, last warning about the noise."

And then Olly moved swiftly and grabbed the Australian by the collar and threatened him with his bulk, his face dead and hostile in the shadow: "Ya fucken show me!" He readied himself to ram his fist into the Aussie's eye socket.

Jack raised his hands and tried to calm him down, going relatively limp in the process. "Okay, okay. Everything's fine, mate." He spoke softly. "Just let me go and I'll bring it up for you."

So he did. And the whole cycle began again, new images emblazoned on his already savaged psyche. Then there was some weeping. And some sitting down. And Jack saying, "Tough break, matey-moo. There, there, eh," in what was a barely passable imitation of giving comfort and providing solace. "Just let it all sink in, mate. In order to move on, first it's gotta get right down deep into your bones so you really hate the bitch. That's an important aspect of the process. Then you won't even care if she's dead and you can just move on with your life. Remember, she's humiliated you in ways that are barely fathomable. She's basically crushed your testicles and sold the video for money. I'm mean, that's pretty much *literally* what she's done." Jack stopped talking and looked up at the moon and then down at its reflected blue glow across the Gulf. It was actually a pretty nice night—an evening for love and poetry. "If I were you, mate, I'd go home and never see her again. Fly back to Limeyland before she does and cut her out of your life. If you can deal with them laughing at you, you could even call the police, see if you can get her prosecuted. Up to you, though." He patted Olly on the shoulder and walked up to the edge of the water and seemed to contemplate it. "Or you could take a long swim. *Really* get out there. The closest island's five clicks. You might be able to make it. Just keep going straight."

It was hard to say whether Olly heard anything Jack had said. He was still sitting blankly in the sand, his focus entirely on a throbbing internalised montage of sex and shouting, of muzzles and humiliation.

Jack looked at him. "Think it over, mate," he said. "Find me tomorrow if you want help flipping your flights around." Then he walked off into the body of the resort, leaving the Englishman to be alone with his collapse.

At some point in the night Olly shuffled down and took up his squatting perch. Adrift in the fleshy shapes of his trauma, he was barely aware of the passing of time.

He was still firmly lodged in this daylight coma when the Murphy twins approached and attempted to make contact, Jason moving in first and bending down, sand bucket still in hand and his blonde hair flopping sideways as he angled himself in order to see Squatting Sad Man's face. "Sad Man!" he said. The Sad Man's eyes were open and red but weren't moving, which was strange, thought Jason, because eyes normally move when they're open. In school Jason had learnt that fish sleep with their eyes open, so it stood to reason that Sad Man might well be a sleeping fish.

"Are you a fish?"

No answer.

"Push him," demanded Matthew, not at all interested in the seemingly random question posed by his brother.

But Jason wasn't going to be goaded into foolishness just yet. There were still tests that needed to be run before they graduated to physicality. "Hello, Sad Man," he said again. But once more the guy did nothing.

"He's frozen," said Matthew.

"No, he's not. He's warm. See. And that means he's not a fish."

Further up the beach and infuriatingly out of earshot, Eleanor watched on nervously as her six-year-old sons put their hands out and touched a strange man who was almost certainly in the grip of psychosis. "I can't fucking believe I let you do this." She gritted her teeth and squeezed her husband's hand. "What the fuck was I thinking? I'm getting them."

Mike pulled her back down. "Just give it a minute."

"Fuck, Mike. This is making me very anxious."

The boys had moved on to scratching their heads in an imitation of studied thought; Jason had even put down his bucket to make sure the problem had his full attention. "Maybe his ears are broken," suggested Matthew. "SAAD MAAAN! CAN YOU HEAR MEEE!?"

He didn't seem to. He just sat there like garden furniture. Best to double the volume. "SAAAD MAAAAN!"

And then Jason joined in. And when that didn't work,

they figured distance was the issue, moved right up to Sad Man's ears—cornering one each to create the full surround sound effect—and squealed in window-shattering fashion. It was the only way to know for sure if Sad Man was truly and profoundly deaf.

"Shit," said Mike.

Eleanor was already up and running.

But suddenly Olly had returned to the world, tumbling backwards out of his strange perch posture and holding his ears and wondering if the drums had well and truly burst.

"Jason! Matthew!" a woman was shouting somewhere beyond the ringing. "Stop it! Leave that man alone."

Olly was coming to himself again as the woman was grabbing two little boys by their arms and apologising. But it was okay.

Everything was fine.

He found himself trying to explain this to the frantic woman. "Nah, it's fine," he was saying.

And the two boys—who hadn't quite registered they were in trouble—were smiling and laughing; they were celebrating the emancipation of Sad Man. They'd won the game, didn't their mother see that? And then she'd dragged them up the beach.

Olly sat for a second and stretched himself out. His legs and arms were sore and he was suddenly very thirsty. His ears felt like they might be bleeding. But it was good. Because nothing obliterates self-important pity like a screaming child. It has the capacity to annex attention and render introspection impossible. And then Olly smiled to himself, his ears still ringing horrifically—as if they had tiny drills inside them—and his body aching. But he felt he had it. The revelation had arrived warm and clear and he knew it was truth. It was the absent factor. And it was why she had been acting out. It was why she'd done everything—the filming, the abuse, her often overly insistent desire to make him a better organiser and thinker. These were just the signals, hardwired into her biology. He simply hadn't been aware enough to catch them—*he hadn't been looking!* Now he knew he had to find her and tell her; he had to make her see that he finally understood, no matter what…

"Sad Man's leaving," Jason said, pointing.

Half seated on the edge of her recliner and waiting for her panic attack to pass, Eleanor was still holding both of her sons' arms—much tighter than she realised. She looked up to find the guy was now standing and wiggling his body around, apparently letting the blood flow back into his limbs. And he appeared to be studying his setting, as if he were trying to place where he was following a burst of unplanned time travel.

"Bye, Sad Man!" Matthew shouted, waving.

The Sad Man smiled and waved back and began to walk off in the opposite direction.

"See," Mike said. "All he needed was the endearing innocence of children in his life."

"Oh *please* shut the fuck up!"

INT. EXECUTIVE OFFICE – DAY

"It's just occurred to me there's quite a bit of dick in this film," says the exec.

"That a problem?" asks the filmmaker.

"Not if it's flaccid… Hey, don't look at me like that. Come on, you know the rules."

"There's a double standard here, and you know it."

"Maybe so, but an unnecessary hard-on crosses a line in terms of gaining any reasonable ratings classification. If it got wide release, quite of few of our markets would want the thing sliced out." The exec makes a snipping gesture with his right hand.

"Neutering my film, huh?"

"Don't look it at that way."

"Hard not to. Look, the professor's erection is thematically important. It's his own little male victory poking into the world. It's a symbol."

"It drags the film down."

"No, it doesn't."

"It spoils things. And that's another issue I'm concerned about. Like the Murphy family—what's even their point in this story? What, are they going to adopt Olly or something?"

"How many times do I have to refer to foils?" the filmmaker says, moderately frustrated. "Binary oppositions. The Murphys represent sane, likeable normality. They exist simply as a point of contrast. That's how painting works, and that's how narratives work."

"I'm worried all these ingredients don't really mix together."

The filmmaker scoffs. "Says the man who won't eat more than one dish at a time."

"Maybe that's why I'm good at this. I just feel I'm hearing some tonal inconsistencies."

"Life's tonally inconsistent."

"Well, of course it is. It's life—it's unedited and ephemeral. That's the *unbearable lightness* Kundera talks about."

"You've read Kundera but not Steinbeck?"

"Comparatively, art is *heavy*," the exec says. "It has to sit there once it's done, suggesting itself, replaying what it has said, remaking its mistakes or recounting its truths for as long as it exists. So unless an artwork's main thematic thrust is the tonal confusion of life, it doesn't really have any business being so itself—especially when people have paid to spend time with it. That's just bad art. It's bad film."

The filmmaker sits morosely for a moment.

"I haven't upset you, have I?" asks the exec, although it's clear that he has.

"For a guy who was just googling images of a woman being fucked by a dog I think you're on a pretty high horse about the duty of art."

"Hey, don't make this about me. Getting *ad hominem* just makes you look bad." The exec pushes his chair away from his desk and stands to look out the window again. "If you're going to be in this business, Max, you've got to be open to criticism. You know that." He turns to look at the filmmaker, who is sitting a little slumped. "Right?"

The filmmaker lingers for a moment before speaking, straightening up as he does so. "Right."

"Did I say I loved the time-lapse idea with Olly paralysed on the beach?"

"No, you didn't."

"Well I do. I think it's fantastic."

"Thank you."

"What happens next?"

INT. RESORT FRONT DESK – MID-AFTERNOON

Jack knew even before Olly came bounding into the empty reception area that he wasn't going to be flying back to England, and it annoyed him. Everything about Olly annoyed him—his face, his ugly tattoo, his swollen arms. But the worst part was his raw stupidity. That was the truly unforgivable aspect—because it meant Jack pitied the guy. It wasn't a nice feeling. And now here he was, loping in like a dog that didn't know it was about to be taken behind the house and shot. Jack imagined walking him into the jungle, having him dig a grave and lie in it while he pointed a gun at his face. Even then Olly would look up with that rudderless perplexity and ask what was happening.

"Good to see you haven't drowned yourself," he said, his tone charred black. "Although that would have been an elegant solution to your problems. You know, there really is an island out there. Full of people taking magic mushrooms—I shit you not." He paused and took a moment to really look at the Englishman. "Mate, are you aware of how sunburnt you are?"

"I need ya help," Olly said. He was trying to look focused, a man in charge of his own destiny.

"I know you do. You wanna change your tickets, yeah? I can get you on a flight out this afternoon. How's that sound to you, big man? Four hours from now and you could be soaring back to the comfort of your mother's ample bosom and reapplying moisturiser to that freakishly parched mug."

"Na, that aint it. I *aint* leavin."

"Of course you're not," Jack said flatly. "Why would you ever do something that sensible?" He tossed his pen on the desk and sighed. "You're a real fucking problem, you know that?"

Olly placed his palms on the desk and leaned in. It appeared he had something big to say, and the fact he looked both left and right before he said it only heightened his cartoonish absurdity. "I'm gonna find er."

"Tell him you disagree and he turns away. Show him facts and figures and he questions your sources. Appeal to logic and he fails to see your point."

"Wat?"

"Festinger. Doesn't matter."

"I want ya ta book me on one-a-them moped tour fings. Same one Soph was on."

"You sure about that? Are you absolutely certain you

don't want me to just get you outta here now? This time tomorrow you could be back in the pub sucking peanuts and complaining about the weather. Doesn't that sound good?"

"I needa find er. I gotta."

Jack dropped his head in resignation. It was important that he slow things down, because unfortunately the contingency plan was now becoming the primary one. Of course, everything that needed to be arranged already had been: the architecture for this particular permutation was well constructed, but now that the Brit was making the choice for real… Well: first it was necessary to let him believe the merits of his course of action were being fully considered—that his path into the future were being carved open by his own freewill rather than being railroaded by the alternative. So, Jack continued, still vaguely hoping that the forces of reason and common sense might dissuade Olly from blundering headfirst into an avoidable oblivion. "Let's say you find her, matey-moo. What's the plan then? You going to chop her into bits and sprinkle her in a river? She won't want to see you. You know that."

"She will."

"She won't, mate."

"She will!" Olly was near violent in his insistence on this point, his eyes glassy and febrile. "I figured it out innit. Everyfing she was doin an like why she was doin it."

Jack didn't bother hiding his scepticism. "Yeah? Go on. Enlighten me."

Again the Brit leaned in, lowering his voice a little in order to conceal his truth, to hide it from possible contamination. "She jus wanned ta ave kids innit."

Jack closed his eyes and tried to imagine somewhere calm. "You're fucking delusional."

"Am not."

"Mate, you could be in a textbook. You're a fucking case study. It's actually painful to see you living and walking around. The depth of your..." He trailed off. What was the point?

"You'll see."

Jack sucked air through his teeth and averted his gaze and tried to repackage things for his client. "So you want to ride a moped up the coast to find the girl who posted non-consensual bondage videos of her bullying and degrading you so that you can suggest having children with her?" He looked at Olly. He didn't seem at all fazed by this summary of the situation.

So be it then, Jack thought. Door's closed. "Okay. I'm going with you. We'll leave tomorrow morning and head up the coast and go town by town. Fuck it, we'll get drunk on the way. Send her a message now and ask where she is. She probably won't reply because you're just a *baffling* dunce, but you never know. And maybe check her Facebook—she might have posted where she is."

"Fanks, Jack." The Australian winced at the sound of his own name. "You're a friend."

"Not really, matey-moo." He scribbled his number on a post-it and slipped it across the desk. "WhatsApp me if you get any info. Otherwise, I'll meet you at your cabin at nine a.m."

He watched Olly leave in a good mood and found himself both infuriated and comforted by it. At least the moron was happy—a man capable of turning denial and self-deception into opiates for difficult times. That had to be something, right? Jack found himself wondering how Pooh Bear might have taken the sort of news Olly had had to digest. Probably would have shot Piglet, then himself… But he'd tried his best with Olly, hadn't he? Certainly there was nothing to be done now: cult-like beliefs are impossible to change, and what's the point in trying to deprogram someone who's not only already spiked their vein with the killer Kool-Aid but is loudly extolling the poison's love and beauty as they choke and die?

Certainly nothing to be done.

And it made him feel better about the Kwan decision, because Kwan was really a last resort kind of option. He took a breath, unlocked his phone, and sent his confirmation message.

Later that afternoon, having finished his shift, Jack returned to his room in the staff accommodation block. Like all the staff lodging it was compact—a single bed, a TV and desk, an *en suite* bathroom and shower, and rather than looking toward the sea (as guest rooms did) its single window was darkened by vegetation, a jungle corner on the fringe of the resort. Sometimes at night macaques scratched against the glass; sometimes he could see snakes coiled in the branches.

He lay down on his bed and switched on the TV. The news was running a story about London, a terror attack, a van mowing people down. A reporter's voice moved monotonously atop helicopter shots of a brown and jagged city. Jack switched the channel and watched *The Simpsons*, closed his eyes, dreamt he was wading up a river infested with cobras, the sky burnt to a dirty yellow. When he woke, it was dusk. He showered, put on a buttoned shirt and rode one of the staff bicycles along to The Strip. He ate *khao man kai* in a back-alley restaurant where the owner knew him, then found a street bar that overlooked the beach so he could drink beer and watch the neon rise into the night. To the north, along the coast, sky lanterns drifted above the trees—a wedding reception at the resort; on the street in front of him tourists mixed with local touts; high-pitched moped engines grated in soft air. The sex clubs were opening—dance music tangling with dance music. Don't strike the bell, he thought; *invite* the bell—a Buddhist fragment he'd picked up. Request the noise and let it in, live with it; if you can do that, it won't bother you. He wondered whether or not this was total shit.

On his fourth beer Kwan's receipt message came through. Just one word.

And now it was official: there was no going back.

No problem. Just *invite the bell*.

He sat for another hour, two phones on the table in front of him, tying off the last of the digital threads. He finished one more beer, paid his bill, and began the cycle back to the resort in the dark. Night riding; beside him the jungle seethed—animals mating and killing.

Back in his room he lay on his bed with the lights off and wondered at the simplicity of it all. At the stupidity. And about his own choices. Would he do this one again? The answer was clear and obvious, utterly unequivocal: of course. For what is life but the adventure of the present, a fleeting opportunity to mould one's reality; a plaything.

His phone began to vibrate. The screen was bright against his eyes. It was Olly, his message clumsy and barely readable: Sophie had updated her location on Facebook—she was now in a town called Duanphen.

INT. EXECUTIVE OFFICE – DAY

"Are we meant to get the impression Sophie's dead?" asks the exec. He's leaning forward. "Also, Olly's really ballooning off the idiot scale here. I mean, kids?"

The filmmaker smiles. "I'll tackle the last part of that first by suggesting you leave your educated bubble of privilege a little more often—not everyone's had the advantages we've had. I guarantee that right now someone is sticking a fork into their toaster or looking down the barrel of their gun wondering why the bullet didn't come out. Olly's just a slow guy under some psychological pressure. And wanting kids in his situation is also rational if you're thinking about the biology of it all."

The exec smirks incredulously. "Biology?"

"He's losing his mating partner, so to speak; his last-ditch effort to keep her would be to try and get her pregnant."

"Hmm." The smirk disappears as the exec considers this. "Come to think of it, that sort of explains my own behaviour after Jenny Forrester left me in college. We would have had such charismatic children." He looks wistful and distant as he puzzles through his memory.

The filmmaker presses on: "As for Sophie, you think she's dead? Is that the impression you're getting?"

The intercom buzzes on the exec's desk before he can answer. He pushes the button allowing him to respond: "Yes, what is it Benny?"

"I have your cup of blood for you, sir."

"Oh. Fantastic. Bring it in." The exec lets go of the button. "Holy shit, right?"

Seconds later the door opens and Benny walks in. He is in his mid-twenties and is extremely well-kept. His hair is carefully parted and his tight-fitting French-grey suit is meticulous. He is carrying a tall glass filled with what looks like dark tomato juice. "Where would you like me to put it, sir?"

"Just on the desk is fine, Benny." The exec watches Benny place the glass on the desk in front of him, then he leans over and looks at it. He seems reluctant to touch it. He looks at the filmmaker, then at Benny. "How long did this take you to get? How long has it been since I asked for this?"

"Fifty-five minutes, sir. Approximately."

"And it's definitely a virgin's blood?"

"Yes, sir. I know you said you didn't need

documentation to verify, but I went ahead anyway and mocked up a certificate of authentication. Would you like to see it?"

"Remarkable!" the exec says, looking closely at the glass. "I can actually smell it—the metallic hint. This is *real* blood!"

"Yes, sir."

"Smell it," the exec says to the filmmaker, although he doesn't follow up on this imperative, instead returning his attention to Benny. The filmmaker notices that Benny manages to stand nearby without actually asserting any sense of physical presence. "And how about budget, how did we do on that front?"

"Given the time constraints of this assignment, sir, I was compelled to use just over $650. I hope that's okay."

"Hell, that's still under budget." The exec turns to the filmmaker. "Didn't I say he was going to come in under budget? Impressive stuff."

"Sure," the filmmaker mutters halfheartedly.

"What? You don't think this is impressive?"

"No, it is, but…"

"What?" The exec twists a little in his chair, facing the filmmaker more directly. "Say what you're thinking, Max."

"It's just… Well, I guess I want it verified, you know. How do I know it's a virgin's blood? Even if it is genuine blood, it could be from anywhere. It could be *cow's* blood."

The exec looks at the filmmaker for a moment in a way that signals true disappointment, and the filmmaker immediately realises his *faux pas*—it's low class to question the veracity of someone else's work when they're standing in the room. The exec, however, decides to be gracious about it and turns his attention to Benny. "I think what Max is curious to know—and I guess I am, too—is the process you went through. How'd you get this stuff?"

Benny shuffles for a moment. "Are you sure you want to know, sir? I feel—and I may be wrong about my brief—but I feel that a good deal of my job is to hide you from the tedious or unpleasant aspects of daily administration."

"In this case, I'm more than sure. Tell us everything you did from the time you received my request to the time you walked in that door and placed this on my desk."

"Yes, sir."

"*All* the details, okay."

"Certainly, sir." Benny closes his eyes for exactly two seconds, accessing it seems a precisely ordered sequence of events. He begins to speak as soon as he opens them, shifting his attention smoothly and evenly between the exec and the filmmaker: "After I received your instructions, I knew I was going to have to be in the office for at least the fifteen minutes it would take for your lunch to arrive, so I used the time to research a few things. First, I looked up where I would be able to buy a cheap, coverall raincoat in the local area—"

"Why?" the filmmaker blurts. "That doesn't—"

"Please, sir, if you'll allow me to explain uninterrupted, the particulars will become relevant in due course."

"Sorry."

"To continue: I searched for nearby outlets where I could buy a cheap, cover-all raincoat. At the same time, not yet sure I would need it but not wanting to be unprepared, I played a tutorial video on how to draw blood. The steps were relatively straightforward, and I only needed half an eye on the screen. I also looked up where I could buy the needles and associated equipment to extract blood, but quickly discovered that this would be difficult within my time window—nothing was close or readily accessible to the common consumer. I also looked up blood donation spots, hospitals, blood storage facilities, and med labs, then calculated the most logistically feasible locations with reference to daytime traffic, as well as a host of other contingencies and variables that I won't bore you with. Then I downloaded and altered a form to use as an authentication certificate, should it become necessary."

"Isn't he a machine?" the exec remarks. He is smiling and listening with rapt attention.

"When your lunch arrived I had it delivered through, then left the building, used the money point on the corner to extract $750 from the company account, then purchased a green raincoat at the Walmart in the commercial park on Vermont Ave. Having put the raincoat on, I walked across the road to the med lab located inside the shopping mall."

"The place where you have swabs and tests done?"

"Yes, sir. Fortunately, the establishment was small, and when I arrived I was the only customer. I immediately asked the on-duty phlebotomist if I could purchase either a 16 or 17-gauge needle and the necessary paraphernalia to extract blood. When he said they weren't for sale I offered $50. He said it wouldn't be ethical since it wasn't his to sell. I said I knew that, and that under normal circumstances I would go to the area's supply outlet directly, but that given my tight schedule it was simply too far away. Then I offered him $100, at which point he said ethics weren't a big thing for him personally, and he gave me the equipment I needed in a brown paper bag that had hitherto contained his lunch. After that I asked if he happened to have the blood of any virgins stored on site, and if so, how much would he sell it for. He then asked me to leave and I did so.

"I then exited the mall and walked back across the parking lot, re-watching the video on how to draw blood as I went. I walked past Walmart and headed for the freestanding Burger King that overlooks the highway, operating largely on the assumption that truant teenagers with nowhere to go tend to find themselves at fast-food restaurants, drawn by the relative security and the free drink refills. Fortunately, my conjectures were correct. Upon entering I immediately spotted three adolescents occupying a booth beside the window. Without preamble—which I find is unnecessary and clouds meaning in strictly transactional matters—I approached the group and explained in very clear terms that I was interested in drawing a unit of blood from one of them, provided they could prove they were a virgin, and that I would give them $500 by way of remuneration. They then made fun of my raincoat, suggested I was a pervert, and tried to ignore me. In response, I showed them the money, at which point they asked if I was serious. I told them I was and removed the necessary equipment from the paper bag to illustrate the fact. I also assured them this had nothing to do with sexual deviance but was, rather, a matter of business that I had been tasked to complete. This matter-of-fact approach engaged them. In my experience, men with sexual motives tend to linger and stare; to avoid this label I thought it best to be impersonal and efficient.

"Once I had their full attention I stressed that it was vitally important the blood came from a virgin. The three then argued among themselves for a few minutes. It seemed that prior to my arrival there had existed within their group a certain level of ego-related fiction regarding sexual experiences. This quickly began to fall away once a financial incentive was involved. They eventually settled on one Rob Ackley—sixteen-years-old—whose sexual totality ostensibly went only as far as fingering a classmate named Sally. I did feel the need at this juncture to censure him for suggesting that Sally's consent to his digital exploration amounted to her being 'loose.' I personally feel it's normal to be curious and sexually active, and I didn't feel she deserved to be judged for it.

"With time a factor, I had Mr Ackley roll up his sleeve while I prepared the equipment. Moving quickly also gave him little chance to back out of the deal or become squeamish. Taking advice from the videos I had watched, I tied his arm off and found a vein, keeping him distracted with banal chit-chat, like suggesting that he should use the money to take Sally somewhere nice—maybe roller skating and the theatre. Ackley then said he wasn't gay or old, so why would he do either of those things. Then I jabbed the needle into his arm and began drawing blood.

"As the bag filled I asked him to sign the certificate of authentication, which, as he started to feel woozy, he did. I told his friends to purchase some food in order to help restore his blood sugar levels, and while they were at the counter, I took advantage of Ackley's momentarily diminished capacity and recorded a video of him on my phone, the needle still in his arm.

"When the blood sack was full and I had 500mls I removed the needle and put all the material back in the paper bag. I thanked all three for their professionalism in the face of what was a deviation from their normal routine, placed $550 on the table, and left. Once back in the office I removed the raincoat, then transferred exactly 250ml into this glass in order to heighten the aesthetic appeal. I have refrigerated the rest of the boy's blood in case you want more for any reason." Benny reaches into his jacket and retrieves his phone and a piece of paper. "Would you like to see the video, sir? Or the certificate?"

"No… But please file both." The exec is looking at the glass again, although he seems somewhat dejected.

"Wait," says the filmmaker. "I still don't get the

raincoat. Was that just a disguise?"

"Is everything okay, sir?" Benny asks his boss, having noticed his expression.

The exec is looking very intently at the glass now. He prods the outside with his index finger, disturbing the stillness of the liquid. "I guess... Maybe it's my fault. No, it's *definitely* my fault. I should have been more specific. I guess when I asked for a virgin's blood I just automatically assumed it would be a girl's. The blood of some slimy teenage boy? Just not as spicy, is it?"

"I'm sorry, sir."

"No, please, don't be. My instructions, my fault."

"Is there anything else I can get you, sir?"

The exec is quiet, still looking at the glass. He flicks it gently with the nail of his middle finger, producing a *tink*. Then another *tink*. "Yes there is, Benny." He looks up at the assistant. "I want a dog. Make it a boy. And I want it big, docile and cute. Extremely cute, if possible. Spend up to $1000 if need be. And I want it this afternoon."

EXT. RESORT, BEACHFRONT CABINS – MORNING

Having slept without nightmares of dismemberment or castration, Olly was in an optimistic mood. He was waiting outside his cabin and sipping from a glass of orange juice when Jack arrived. The day was clear and blue and already hot—woven, it seemed to Olly, with the promise of success. "We're gonna find er," he said, as if she were a grail. "I kin *feel* it."

Jack looked at the Englishman sitting there in the sun: only the intellectually feeble could be truly earnest about anything, divested as they were of worries about clichés and platitudes, incapable of feeling like buffoons. They weren't ashamed of their emotions. But was that lack of shame a weakness or a strength? Jack imagined Olly defecating with a serious look on his face, then had to shake the image before he could speak. "You're a man with conviction, mate," he said. "A lot of people would admire that. Not sure I do, though."

"Why ya such a nega-iv guy?" Olly asked.

The question surprised Jack. He hadn't held Olly in high enough regard to think him capable of making an observation, let alone asking a follow-up question about it. "I don't know. I like to think of myself as one of the happier people I know," Jack said. "So that's really a matter of perception."

"Whaddya mean?"

"Well, for instance, take your glass of O.J. there." Olly looked at it; examined it. Jack continued: "You, no doubt, would claim it's half full, whereas I look at it and wonder how difficult it would be for me to piss in it, then get you to drink it. Ya see what I'm saying?"

"Not really."

"It's the way I was raised, I guess." Jack turned in the direction of the beach and spent a few seconds breathing quietly, his hands in his pockets, squinting out at the water. He put his sunglasses on. "Come on, matey-moo. We're gonna do great things today."

It was only chance that meant Eleanor Murphy saw the two of them leave, helmets on, T-shirts flapping as their mopeds accelerated out the back gate of the resort. By all rights, she shouldn't have been there at all, but while sitting at breakfast with her family a sudden and almost crippling urge to smoke a cigarette had overcome her. Having scurried away on a bathroom pretext, she'd bummed what she needed from a maintenance worker for far too many *baht*, then shuffled out a rear exit.

She wasn't at all sure where the urge had come from; she hadn't smoked since she was a teen and was well aware it was a filthy habit that her husband in particular disapproved of. Maybe, she thought as she inhaled vigorously, bestial and semi-squatting near a phalanx of back-gate dumpsters, this was her hedonic treadmill finally kicking it up a notch. She'd graduated to the next level of need, and it was manifesting itself by rekindling a dormant desire for nicotine.

Then the strange thing happened. While dealing with the sudden headrush and a sickness in her stomach, the two mopeds passed her, stopping for a moment as Jack punched in an exit code and the gates opened, and it was in that time that Olly, with his bike idling, turned his head and looked at her. And seemed to recognise her. And he found himself waving, which she reciprocated with a wave of her own from her awkwardly crouched position, lifting and bending her frame to straighten herself in a way that should have been completely routine, but while light of mind and queasy of body the movement somehow had all the confounding complexity of copying down numbers in a dream. She wondered what it looked like from the outside. And she felt very strange all of a sudden, caught in something cold, and she felt the urge to shut her eyes tight, to squeeze hard and wring the chill from them.

Then the gates opened and the mopeds took off with their chainsaw engines, and Eleanor had to hold on to the side of the dumpster to keep from falling over, the sound itself threatening to rip her in two. She threw the cigarette to the ground and tried to reacquire control of herself. She tried to take a breath, long and deep, but instead of taking fresh air, she took the smouldering remains of the butt as it persisted on the concrete beneath her, and the pungent waft of rotting food waste in the morning heat, and an errant parachute of phlegm that caught the verve of her inhalation and exploded in her windpipe. The resulting coughing fit was guttural and demonic.

Having clambered back inside she nearly stumbled into her own table. "Easy," said Mike without looking up.

"I just saw that guy again," she said. Her eyes were watering.

Mike was nibbling on toast and drinking coffee as he read a newspaper. "Who?"

"Sad Man. I had the weirdest feeling."

"Sad Man!" Jason said, waving his spoon.

"Weird how?"

"Just… Unsettling. I don't know. It was like a portent."

"Nice word." Mike was simultaneously reading Dilbert and had yet to look up. "What was he doing?"

"Riding out of the place on one of those scooter things with some other guy."

"That's good. He's making friends. Maybe he's gay. Is that what you found unsettling? My wife the giant homophobe."

"I can't really explain this, but… Looking at him was like watching something fall out of the sky dead…"

Mike retreated from his paper, having finally registered the off tone in Eleanor's voice, and looked at her. She seemed a little shell-shocked; her eyes and face were red. "Are you okay?"

"Just, I don't know. A bit freaked out for some reason."

He started sniffing. "Why do you smell like cigarette smoke?"

Olly had no such unsettling sense. Quite the reverse. As he sped along the open road he felt himself being lifted from his troubles. Movement was what he had needed all along—the blur of roadside attractions, rundown clothing stores, dilapidated hotels, cafés that looked like they were a gentle breeze away from falling over: he pulled beyond it all, motion synonymous with escape from himself and the torment of the past few days. For the first time he was truly seeing the country, registering its fundamental difference to the stolid grind of South London. He was in the subtropics, and it was green and hot and wet all at once. Elephant signs; elephant statues; long threading nests of powerlines wilted by the humidity; the inscrutable form of Thai script painted on boards, on shop fronts, like psychedelic musical notes. And beyond them the hills climbed and met marble clouds; jungle assertions and curling mysteries. Olly followed Jack as he accelerated around cars, overtaking in narrow gaps and pushing ahead and forcing Olly to recklessly do the same. They began to ascend. The roads started to hook and bend in ways that didn't seem possible, buildings disappearing as jungle took over and they found themselves riding through long glades, sun and shade dappled, the canopy opening into cliffsides and death drops. But even as the road became severe Jack seemed to pick up speed, careening blindly into sharp corners, at one point swerving to avoid an oncoming van, and Olly tried his best to keep up, twisting the accelerator and red-lining the engine so that it screamed its way up and onward.

By eleven they were deep in the hills, their bikes parked outside a roadside café, drinking their first beer of the day and looking at a view that rippled across a lush landscape toward the sea. Once again Olly thought it was right to thank Jack, to show his appreciation for everything he'd done in the aftermath of his difficulties. "Please, mate," Jack had replied. "You need to shut up. I really don't want to talk about feelings. Just live in the present. You know what that means?"

"Yeah," Olly said. He knew this one. "Like, preciate where ya are an wat ya doin, innit?"

"Nice one, fella. Good for you. Do that." Jack smiled at him, and for a moment the smile seemed genuine rather than a hostile facsimile. Maybe it *was* genuine.

They rode on, down into the jungle, a tumbling green kaleidoscope churning in the urgency of the day. Even against the hum of the bikes Olly could hear the birds and the life. They passed elephants—live ones, real ones, elephants with tusks and trunks. They swam at an empty beach where the water was clear and the sand unspoiled. They rode again. Olly felt salt on his forearms as the sun pressed against them, his hands contently gripping the bike and steering it along a coastal road that had narrowed to a single lane. Dogs in light, barking as he passed; flimsy docks built out into the water; longtail boats static beside his own momentum. They had lunch at a beachside eatery—rice from leaves, more beer—then pushed on again: another stop to watch the Gulf water, another beer, another stretch of rustic pavement.

Jack slowed his bike and stopped.

They'd been weaving inland and back out again, through shanties and fishing villages where children walked barefoot on the dirt edge and livestock seemed to roam free. The middle of nowhere. Jack waited, switched off his moped. Olly did the same, the sound of the jungle filling the void left by the absence of the engines. "Wait here a moment," Jack said, and then he disappeared along a tight track, leaving Olly to himself and the bird sounds.

The stereo howling of faceless monkeys.

The scent of rich wet dirt.

And then his thought about the fact he hadn't thought about Sophie for a number of hours broke his spell. He wondered how she would have felt about him today—if she could have seen him. He felt cool. Intrepid on his little bike, carving his way into the unknown. Would she respect him?

And then he thought about her hitting him. The slapping and punching. The leather stench of the muzzle. And for the first time the significance of it all registered with something inside him: the fundamentals had finally made it through the bureaucratic tangle of his emotions and denials and been fully cognitively received. The resulting anger came through like diamond lightning.

"Come on," Jack said, reappearing abruptly. "Follow me."

Olly looked up and tried to shake off the thoughts. "Where we goin?"

"Surprise, matey-moo." Then Jack disappeared back up the track.

Olly did as he was told and trailed behind, watching where he placed his feet as the track got tighter. The vegetation began brushing against his shoulders, then he looked up and the path had opened to a clearing in which stood a small wood-panelled building, its navy paint inconsistently applied. A Thai man was standing in front of the screen door. He looked middle-aged. He was wearing sandals and a baggy singlet that fully illustrated the bones in his shoulders. The scars on his arms and face were hard to ignore, the scar tissue itself purple in the shade of the surrounding jungle. "Nī pĕn h̄eyùx k̄hxng khuṇ h̄rūx mị̀?" The voice was musical and totally confounding.

"Chì," said Jack.

"Wat 'e say?" Olly asked.

"What *did* he say. Your syntax is awful. He asked if

you were the victim."

"Wad you say?"

"I said yes." A fixed smile.

Jack spoke to the man again in Thai and the man laughed and waved his hand in a motion to follow him. "Wat's goin on?" Olly asked. He was recognising an old feeling—a slug was being mutilated in the flame of a lighter, turning black and bubbling.

"Mate. Be cool. You'll love this. You'll be the envy of all your tragic limey friends." The smile remained and it made Olly uncomfortable.

"I fink ya should tell me wat's goin on…"

Jack stopped and turned around. "Look, this guy's an old friend, and he's doing me a favour—*a favour I've had to pay for*—so stop being a massive ukulele and come the fuck along."

The tiger was in a shabby wire cage at the back of the building. The cage was the size of a small bedroom, its concrete floor darkly stained, the animal sleeping right in the middle. Olly watched its huge ginger coat rising and falling with its breath. "Beats Tiger Kingdom, am I right?" Jack was grinning.

"Tiger Kingdom?"

"It's where posers go if they wanna finger a heavily tranquilized tiger and take a selfie. But what's the point in that? Where's the regal bloodlust of a genuinely hungry predator. Am I right?" Before Olly had taken the animal in, the Thai was opening the door and saying something in his sing-song language, and Olly found himself backing away instinctively, his body shaking, his hands straining and twitching in what felt like the precursor to a debilitating fit of panic and pure terror. "Wat's 'e doin?"

"Easy, mate. He's a pro. He's done this before."

"Fuck."

The man continued babbling (to himself or to Jack or to the tiger, it was impossible for Olly to know) but as he did so he picked up a long bamboo shaft and began prodding the tiger through the wire, then he turned to Jack and pointed to a spot: "Yūn xyū̀ thỉ nỉ."

Jack moved to where he'd been told. With the cage door open he was in the direct path of the tiger, and now the owner was jabbing the beast awake, agitating it with pokes to its ribs, its eyes opening. "Mate!" Olly blurted, and almost instantly the cat lunged forward, its body thick with muscle, its growl rending the air as it moved. And as it fled the open cage and swiped at Jack—a swipe with all the power and claw to disembowel—it snapped hard on the chain attached to its rear leg and jerked back, the chain itself wincing with the tension. It was a feature Olly hadn't noticed in the flood of fear and adrenaline. The tiger growled again, and in the wall of the jungle it resounded as a primal echo, triggering the flight of birds and the screams of primates. The big cat's teeth were slick and ready for meat.

Jack squatted near it, watched it move. "See, fella. Guy's a pro." He turned and looked at Olly. "Come on over. Get as close as you can."

Olly moved in, a bit at a time, flinching at the growl, his nervous system electrocuted. He hunched down next to Jack, trying not to display how frightened he was. Then the tiger swiped again and he fell back, instinct overriding everything. "Calm down, you blouse," Jack said. "Just look into its eyes. Sit where I'm sitting. See if you can stare it down. Ya gotta let it know you're looking at it. Pull that off and it'll let you into the mystical water garden of naiads and champagne. You just have to look for the emerald inside its pupil."

"Emerald?"

"The tiny flash of supernatural green hiding in the dark of its eye. See that shit and you see everything."

"Everyfing," Olly repeated.

From behind the cage Jack zoomed in and took photos while Olly tried to muster the courage to antagonise the animal as it strained against the full length of its chain. "Get right in there, mate. Remember: it's just a tiger." From Jack's point of view, it almost looked as if Olly were trying to hypnotise the thing, his eyes tracking the animal's with comedic intensity. Every now and then the owner bashed on the side of the cage with the bamboo, vibrating a thin wire rattle atop the tiger's roar—a sound that seemed to irritate the cat as it gnashed and snarled at the Englishman and pulled at the integrity of its flimsy restraint. "Chạn hı̄wạng wā sò nî ca mī khûn," the Thai said to Jack, thwacking the cage again, his purple facial scars twitching obsessively.

Jack shrugged and took another photo. "If it breaks,

it'll be a cool way for him to die."

Olly caught none of this exchange. He was too occupied, gazing into the snarling face of the beast, scanning, hunting, searching—though he remained unsure what he was meant to be seeing. It was hard for him to get close enough to see much in the pupils beyond the inevitability of being mauled to death, but he was getting as close as his survival instinct would allow, the beast pulling up onto its hind legs and trying to reach out and bat his skull as if it were a ball of yarn. And that growl. The growl was a kind of meat cleaver, hacking away at the outer flesh and leaving organs open to the air, spilling to the dirt.

INT. EXECUTIVE OFFICE – DAY

"I need to stress how important it is to have a *real* tiger," says the filmmaker. He is looking keenly at the exec. "This can't be a CGI cheat."

"I understand that," says the exec. "I was thinking the same thing."

"It's not a matter of verisimilitude. I fully appreciate the capacity of high-quality CGI to create something that is visually indistinguishable from the real product. But that's the thing—in the end, it's not about the visual component. It's the essence. And the audience have an extra-sensory perception about this stuff. Unless it's actually there, they'll instinctually know that this tiger can't be hungry, can't panic, and can't maul."

"I agree."

"Computer generated is shorthand for non-existent. It means shadows, ghosts. At best, you get surreal dreams. But this tiger—even though it's caged and being jabbed with sticks—it must represent the fundamentals of life and death. The passion and violence. It has to *stink* of death. It has to be real."

"I'm with you, Max. One-hundred percent all the way." The exec reaches out and carefully moves the glass of blood to the edge of his desk.

EXT. DERELICT RURAL BEACHFRONT – AFTERNOON

The two men sat drinking by the beach in a rundown pagoda, the red tiles on its roof mostly faded to pink or else missing altogether. The wind had picked up and was blowing hot and ragged across the water, and now that it was mid-afternoon the sun seemed to swirl. Olly was still juiced from his face-to-face with the jungle monster, propped up on one of the structure's peeling walls and tapping his bottle in an energetic rhythm. "Ow come that guy's allowed ta keep a tiger like that?".

"Allowed? Jesus, Olly. Did he look like someone who diligently applies for permits?"

"And ow come I aint know you could chat Taiwanese?"

Jack chose not to correct the Englishman, though he

needed to swig from his beer to suppress the urge. "Mate, we've been through this: you don't know anything about me."

Olly narrowed his eyes, not sure this was entirely true… "Yeah, I do. I know a few fings."

"Nah, mate. Ya don't."

"I know that–"

"Woah there." Jack stood and moved from the shade of the pagoda. "We're not gonna wander down the path of you telling me that you know I'm Australian or some shit like that." He finished his beer and threw the bottle over the sand and into the water and immediately grabbed a fresh one from his bag. "Fact is, you don't know anything about me. Now that's mostly because you're going through some personal turbulence, so asking polite questions about other people hasn't been a top priority. As such, I'm not too offended by the social shortcoming." He popped his new beer open with the edge of his cell phone, apparently unconcerned by the damage the cap's serration inflicted on the screen. "But what troubles me is the staggering ease with which you trust people. Totally unquestioningly. Blindly. Dumbly. That could get you into lots of shit. Fuck, mate—it already *has*. I imagine if you'd grown up in a less fortunate country you'd already be bone meal. Probly would've been raped first, too."

"Sorry," Olly said. He took a moment to think, the bending heat stirring in his vision. "Yeah, sorry, mate." He suddenly felt extremely bad for not having asked questions, for having ignored who this guy was—someone who'd helped him when things went sideways and who was with him now even though he probably had somewhere better to be. "Should've asked about ya," he said, dipping his head in shame, then lifting it again to impart vital feelings: "Ya been real elpful. You're a mate. I know that. A top lad."

Jack pulled on his beer and looked up the coast and into the wind; it stretched interminably into the distance, like a bent arm—flesh into a hazy horizon. Whitecaps were starting to form as gusts tugged at the water. "Olly…" He looked over at the Brit—the forlorn eyes, the puppy trust. "You enjoying the ride today? Like, you enjoying the day?"

Olly smiled; it was an easy question. "It's bin wicked innit. Bin sick. Foreal, like, the best since I got ere."

"Not much of a contest though, eh."

"Nah, mate." He shook his head. "But just gettin in em 'ills. Ridin. And that *fuckin tiger*! Man, fuckin unreal!"

"You know, matey-moo, there aren't many people I've taken to see that tiger."

"Foreal?" Olly said. "So, I'm gettin the full tour?"

"That you are my organ bank." Jack toasted him and took another drink, then turned again and wandered toward the water's edge.

Olly looked out at the Gulf, then pulled himself around to stare into the mountains, then at the mopeds. He was taking everything in, tasting the air, understanding the light. It was all settling and making sense. This was a place he could live, he thought. And Jack's off-camber smile: that was the grin of freedom. That's why it had seemed sinister—because it was the opposite of slate-sad London and his mates and the concrete world of jobs and toil. It was the smile of a guy who played with tigers and sped through mountain traffic and spoke a weird foreign language. And what was stopping Olly from just quitting the UK and doing what Jack did, getting some easy job and living? "Yeah, serious like..." he called, raising his voice into the breeze. "Ow come you can speak Taiwanese? Ya learn it in school?"

Jack took his time before turning and answering, actively finishing his beer, draining the bottom half in one long foamy swallow, then firing it into the scrubland behind them. He opened another, again utilising the edge of his cell phone, and swallowed from that, too. "Ya really wanna know?"

"Yeah, mate."

"You know what a missionary is?"

"Lad's on top, girl's underneef."

"If only, right!" Jack belched aggressively, although he managed to continue speaking right through it. "Nah, mate. I feel if my mum had enjoyed the sex act more she wouldn't have spent six months a year trying to hook strangers on the love of Christ inside a sticky Buddhist jungle. She was a kind of spiritual drug dealer. But, you know, getting high on her own supply and all that."

Olly followed none of this. "Ya mum sold drugs?"

"She was a Christian, Olly. Loved Jesus. And she wanted other people to love Jesus, too. Especially people who were already quite happy with their own alternative version of Jesus. And she did that here a lot when I was growing up. Which is why I have both Australian and Siamese tongues."

"You gotta twin?"

"Nah, mate." Jack smiled. "You know, talking to you is a bit like being stoned. But the more I drink the less I find that annoying."

"Wait…"

"I lived here a lot as a kid," Jack clarified. "So, I speak the language. And I have no brothers or sisters."

"So, no twin…?

"No, Olly."

Olly played with his beer, rolling it around in his hands, ruminating with his palms. "Ya fink I could live ere?" It seemed like he was asking for permission. "Like, ow ard would it be for me to move ere?"

"Why? You wanna come work at the resort? Apply your problem-solving skills to the leisure industry? Guess we could just oil you up and leave you by the pool, call you an aesthetic perk."

"Sorta, yeah."

"Dunno if that gels with your notion of having kids with the witch, matey-moo." Jack chugged away the bottom half of his beer and immediately grabbed another. He was now well ahead of the Englishman, who was still nursing his first. "Speaking of which, witch, which, we're gonna have to skedaddle shortly if we wanna rendezvous with the Sophinator." He took a drink. "You know,

Olly—*broski*—I gave you a ton of shit for sticking by her and wanting her back. And sure, I still think it would have been better for you to have just fucked off back to Big Ben when I recommended it rather than clinging to your quote-unquote feelings, but hey, whatever. Despite what I said, I sort of *do* admire your loyalty. If the American public had had that kind of loyalty, Vietnam would be like Mississippi right now. Anyway, it's something! It's arguably a positive character trait, is what I'm saying." Jack's voice was getting louder and looser as the rapid succession of beers began to work on him. "And I kind of think that sort of trait is in your blood. Gotta be, right? Probably fused into your DNA... You know, you hear stories about, like, some unpleasant penis who's dying of heart failure. Then some agreeable shmucko gets hit by a truck while saving a baby or something stupid, and the penis ends up getting the shmucko's heart in a transplant. After that the penis is suddenly all nice to his wife and kids, starts lowering the interest on the loans he gives out—you know, starts tryna be a *pleasant* penis instead of a *cunt* penis. And everybody's like, wow, it must be that shmucko's heart he's got in his chest—the shmucko's holistic goodness is seeping out into the penis's bloodstream." Jack stopped for a moment before pointing directly at Olly and continuing with force: "Problem is, this penis guy has spent his whole life ejaculating on people and thus creating the kind of culture around him in which being a prizewinning fuckhole is actually vital to survival, and now that he's good, he's all flaccid and kickable, right? So his kids and his wife start walking all over him, and everyone defaults on their loans knowing they can get away with it, and so he dies bankrupt and with his floppy purple corona being knifed into the dirt by the very people he's tried to help... Ya get me?"

A gust of wind pulled up sand from the beach and peppered it indiscriminately across the metal road beyond the shore. The Australian drained the rest of his beer and tossed the empty. Olly found himself captivated by the sonorous plonk the bottle made as it landed in the scrub. "So," Jack said. "Let's get outta here, yeah?" He turned to face the beach and started urinating, the rising wind fraying the integrity of his stream and spritzing his hands. "Gotta go find ya woman!"

"I don't fink I wanna see er."

Jack didn't hear this. He kept talking and pissing. "Duanphen's about twenty minutes ride from here and we're on a tight schedule. Gotta be surgical with this stuff. Clinical. Seek exactitude, Olly." He zipped up and moved to grab his backpack. "An' if I drink too much more I'll be Aussie paste on a palm tree, so—"

"Mate!" Olly shouted. Jack found himself looking up in bewildered surprise, halfway through zipping up the main pocket. "I don't fink I wanna see er." Olly shook his head and sipped his beer. He hadn't even moved from his perch on the wall of the pagoda. "I fink you was right about er."

"What?"

"Yeah, like, I know it's taken me a bit an everyfin,

but… she fuckin used me!" He was finally clear on this point. Olly could feel the virulence of his sunburn reassert itself as Sophie's existence invaded his language. "An when I fink about her now, I get angry, so I don't fink I wanna see er. Like ya said, just cut er out, right?" He looked expectantly at Jack for approval of his feelings. But the Australian hadn't moved, his bag still half closed, his thumb and index finger still on the zip. "…Right?"

"Fuck, Olly."

"It just makes sense to me now innit. Specially ridin today. I was just sat here finkin it's been good. Just me an you. Dint ave to take no photos or nuffink. Dint get slapped. It's been good innit? Couldnta done none of that wiff Soph."

"Fuck, Olly. Fuck, mate." Jack dropped the backpack on the ground, then immediately returned to it for another beer, which he fumbled to open with his phone, this time gouging his finger in the movement—although he didn't seem to register the pain, instead drinking first and then sucking at the blood. "I really wish you'd fucking told me sooner."

It wasn't clear to Olly why Jack was angry. "I'm sorry I changed me mind, mate—but, like, I was finkin bout what ya said, an you're real smart. Like, what kinda koala needs a balloon with acid n shit in it…? Mate?"

But Jack was already walking away with his drink to be alone on the beach, striding off as if distance might solve the problem. He pulled up at the water's edge and swore into the air. Then he swore again.

Because flip-flopping now was *not an option*—not at this late stage when the plans were concrete, fully networked—a constellation of interests all tangled together and knotted in such a way that they could not be unpicked. There was no going back! The wind blew against his face: "We're already in the cluster, matey-moo!" Nothing would go awry. Nothing. These things were fixed: Kwan says so. Implacable, immutable, irre-fucking-versible. What's done is *very* done and therefore without all fucking regard and FUCK!

"FUCK!"

Jack became aware that he was shouting on the beach, that his actions were both audible and visible to the man waiting by the bikes. He tried to compose himself, to shake out the beer and find the necessary equanimity to deal with the problem.

Breathe in.

Watch the ocean. Hear the wind.

Breathe out.

Now return and face the situation.

"Ya okay?" Olly asked. He'd climbed down from the pagoda and looked genuinely concerned as Jack wandered in from the sand. "Whas wrong?" The sincerity in those dragging syllables was crippling.

"Yeah, mate. It's just…"

"Wat…?"

Jack played with the hair on his crown and rubbed his neck. "Mate, it was supposed to be a surprise."

"Wat?"

"Well..." He dropped his head for a moment, then held up his phone. "I was in touch with Sophie this morning. She's in Duanphen now. She communicated to me that she wants to have you back and that she's sorry she's been a massive bitch." Jack looked at Olly's face. It was twisting in the golden light, yet to fully register meaning. "She said that she wants to try again. Basically, she's done some soul-searching feminine shite and wants to be a better version of herself for you. Anyway, she's in Duanphen now. She's gonna meet us at a bar I know. I'm supposed to ride you there, then I was gonna leave you guys to it."

Olly looked around himself. Watching him from a distance it would have seemed like he'd dropped something, like his keys had fallen in the grass. Jack finished his beer and weighed up whether or not to add more, whether saying something about having kids would be a step too far.

Olly lifted his head and squinted again, one eye closing more than the other. "Wad she say, like on the phone?"

Jack shrugged. "She said she'd had some time to think about what you meant to her and how much you did for her—stuff like that. And how she's willing to change for you. She wants to treat you with respect and as an intellectual and social equal."

"Don't sound nuffink like Soph."

"Mate, I'm paraphrasing." He examined the Englishman's face as he tossed his empty. "When she said it, it sounded more like her."

Olly was still squinting, his expression locked tight as he worked everything through. In the end, however, the thinking was cursory—a formality in the rush to a decision that had truly been made in the instant new information had been revealed. Because neither the anger he'd felt standing in the jungle nor the crystallisation of his resolve had been established long enough to withstand the sudden wonderful onslaught of everything he'd wanted. A new and improved Sophie was in Daunphen. Fact. And the revelation was so aggressively tidal, so total and all-consuming, that his brief flirtation with personal integrity was simply washed over and destroyed; in less than a moment, it was as if it had never existed.

Jack watched as this change bore itself out on Olly's face: the twitch of the nose, the unfurrowing of the brow, the mouth opening just a shade. "Sorry I kept it from ya, fella. She was very insistent on the nature of the surprise."

"S'okay," Olly said, although he was now struggling to hold in his enthusiasm. "This's a real good day, innit?"

"Ya happy?"

He nodded. "Yeah, mate." He looked out at the coastal light, eyes shimmering, a muscular totem of sudden personal ecstasy, then he turned and stepped forward and enveloped Jack in a strong hug of love and gratitude, and Jack could feel Olly's heart thumping in his chest and the convulsions of honest emotion, and he could taste the acrid citrus of the bigger man's sweat as he started weeping.

"Easy, matey-moo," he said, taking Olly by the shoulders and carefully trying to disentangle himself. "There, there. Let's reign that in. No need for an unseemly forward rush of sentiment." The Englishman had the unthinking smile of a man totally overcome, and Jack found it difficult to look at. "Let's celebrate this in a more traditional fashion." He reached into the jumble of his backpack and felt around for more beer. "We'll do this properly. A toast to celebrate your new success, and to your happiness. That's the *right* thing to do." He handed Olly an open drink.

"Fanks." He sponged away the last of the tears with the hem of his singlet.

Even as the guy blubbered, Jack was struck by the fact he looked like an underwear model, the banal and slightly snotty incarnation of an advert for boxers or briefs. "Stop your sniffling, mate. This is to you and your future." He held his drink up. "But as soon as we've polished these, we're riding like the Roadrunner. Don't wanna keep the lady waiting."

Olly stood straight, aligning his spine to his renewed sense of purpose and dignity, and lifted his own drink. His mind was clear and he was ready. "Cheers."

The bottles clinked. Waves broke across the shore.

EXT. SWIMMING POOL – AFTERNOON

Eleanor sat up from her lounger in a frozen sweat. "God. I just had an awful feeling."

For a change, the family were poolside rather than on the beach, having decided it was important to utilise the resort's actual facilities before winging back to Chicago.

"Maybe you should have a cigarette then." Mike turned the page of his *New Scientist*. He was in the middle of an article about the mercurial nature of personal identity, and although he found it dull, he didn't want to be beaten by it.

Eleanor watched the twins splash in the pool. She couldn't shake it. "Like a sudden sense of horrible apocalyptic dread." She rubbed her arms. "Like it's started raining body parts. The sky's just opened up and out come all these limbs. Human meatgrinder…" The twins were slapping the water with their palms. "I feel cold…"

"Definitely smoke a cigarette then."

The twins continued slapping the surface, hands flat against the tension.

**EXT. A DIFFERENT SWIMMING POOL –
AFTERNOON**

Approximately sixty kilometres away, nestled in a manicured jungle clearing and with a panoramic view of the mountains, Sophie was also sitting beside a swimming pool. She was in her bikini, painting her toenails vermillion and drinking something that resembled a cosmopolitan, though wasn't quite. She'd decided Quack (not his actual name) wasn't a particularly good barman, but at least he was better than Fuck-Suck (ditto) who didn't even speak English and seemed pretty dim. Fuck-Suck spent most of the day standing out front by the car waiting to go somewhere, just letting flies land on him.

    She continued to carefully apply the nail polish to her left pinkie. When she was done she would get Quack to blow on them.

Since her arrival in Thailand, everything had gone just as she'd been told it would, and her part had been mostly straightforward. She'd felt a little bad about Olly, of course—he wasn't supposed to have turned up like that—but she felt she'd met the challenge in a professional and realistic manner by smashing him with a chair and running off. If anything, it added to the cover story. And frankly it was his fault for being a moron. If he'd been smarter—that is, from the very beginning of his time with her—nothing bad would ever have happened. The fact it had: well, that was just natural law: cattle become burgers, chickens become drumsticks, lobsters get boiled alive. In the end, the Thailand job had dovetailed nicely with her need to let him go. He'd done his duty, serving as much purpose in her life as he was ever going to. She was on to better things. Time to let him fly.

She comforted herself with the notion that he might meet someone more his speed back in London, someone who would love him and might actually desire his company. In his own way, she thought, he would've made a passable father. Attractive, relentlessly sweet, strong arms for pushing a pram around a park. Absolutely malleable. And who wants a guy who's smarter than them anyway?

She shook the image from her mind before it managed to get its barbs into anything soft, then picked up the magazine that was lying to her right and did one of the lines of cocaine piled on its cover. Returning to the task of her nails, she actively thought of Olly muzzled, mumbling and struggling to speak. She thought of punching him in the face and of grabbing his cheek while she rode him, pulling it hard and seeing that look of fear on the other side of his sunglasses.

Affection was an easy sentiment to purge.

It was the morning after she'd broken a chair on his head that she'd vacated the resort, walking up the road, as instructed, and waiting beside a sign with an elephant on it. In no time at all, a green hatchback had pulled up, and out jumped a Thai man in his thirties, opening the back door for her as if she were foreign royalty. Within an hour she'd been driven to the villa, where she was told to make herself at home. Everything was private—the lawn and pool, the mountain views—and everything was free: the drugs, the alcohol, the food, all of which would be prepared for her whenever she desired. Of course, there could be no internet, Quack apologised. But that was part of the deal and would ensure overall security.

"Well wa'the fuck am I s'pposda do then?"

Quack recommended the drugs, the alcohol, the sun. The pool was good by day, the jacuzzi by night.

She took his advice and did it all, maxing herself out on MDMA and champagne, working on her tan, swimming naked as the drugs went to school on her brain and she lost any real sense of where she was or what she was doing. It was her holiday, after all—a working holiday, yes, but still a time to unwind.

The rest of her luggage arrived the second day, hauled

in by Fuck-Suck as she lay splayed and semi-conscious by the water. She lifted her head in partial acknowledgment and wondered absently whether she should seduce Quack, then nodded off.

The only real hardship was her social media. It had been part of the deal, though—something to do with geolocations and smooth evidentiary narratives. She'd had to give him her phone. So: No Facebook. No Instagram. No messages to or from friends back home.

Digital detox.

Without something to scroll through she found herself looking around at things, listening. But the drugs helped. All the good times happen when you're high and naked and screaming monkey noises into an amphitheatre of jungle, the monkeys screaming back.

By day three she didn't even miss her cell. Of course, she had everything else she needed. Quack fed her and watered her; she watched TV; she threw things at Fuck-Suck and ingested chemicals all day, then a sleeping pill at night to rebalance. She found herself forgetting her other life entirely. A crimson sun diving into the trees, her brain expanding and contracting, swelling, constricting—she was smiling. She was making out with Quack (he wasn't so bad) her feet in the pool, birds taking crepuscular flight. And the set-up to all of it seemed so long ago—so full of details that didn't seem entirely relevant anymore. Easiest money of your life, the Australian had said. *Fun* money.

Nothing to regret. Just in and out.

She felt the sun crisp her skin; the wet lasciviousness

of liberation south of the equator. The sky in this place had shades it didn't have elsewhere; a mind built of watercolours, fingers dipped in and pulled across a canvas.

A holiday.

Was Quack taking photos of her poolside? Maybe. Hard to say.

And then she was painting her nails vermillion—maybe because that was the colour she'd seen in the sky—sipping pseudo-cosmopolitans and jacking line after line of cocaine from the cover of an Asian Vogue. She wasn't quite sure what day it was anymore, but it didn't seem to matter. Quack would keep her up-to-date on developments, let her know when time was time and when work needed to be work. And she would take his suggestions: a quick swim, a small salad, a spoonful of MD…

He was blowing the polish dry on her toes. The air from his lips was smooth and constant, and he was holding her foot very gently—as if it were porcelain—his silhouette barely distinguishable against the flicker of the dusk, the butterflies, her radically dilated pupils. She said something—something about the light and the drugs, she wasn't quite sure—and then he replied that it was indeed time. That over the next hour, she would have to follow his instructions very carefully. "Take my hand, Miss Sophie, and I will help you dress and prepare you for your journey. We have been given our instructions."

She nodded and smiled, unable to fully control the movement of her neck.

INT. EXECUTIVE OFFICE – DAY

"Now imagine we're holding this shot on Sophie's face, her eyelids heavy, the frame floating around her. This is a *subjective* camera. It's her reality, and outside her face, which is drifting away into a sweet and surreal inebriation, everything is Gaussian soft, or bokah, or impressionistic— it really doesn't matter, as long as it's tripped into a warm psychedelia. And the sounds around her, it's like they've been soaked—the sound of her voice saying *okay*, and this is the only time in the film we're going to really be lost in its musicality, soothed by it. This is audio-visual honey to represent how much she's taken, okay? The song that had been playing diegetically from the house, it's invading during this section. Think something like *MGMT*—you know, that whole woodland acid-rave vibe; pixies and nymphs and *A Midsummer Night's Dream*? The aural equivalent of a lot of hot friendly people rubbing each other with various body paints and glitters. That's the sound that's taking over at this point. That's Sophie's *subjective* reality."

The exec nods. "Great," he says. He's got his hands back in the triangle of thought and power, his elbows on the desk as he leans in. There is rain hitting the window, but neither he nor the filmmaker has noticed it.

"Then the camera begins to pull out, almost as if it's being dragged very slowly by some angelic force, up into the sky—still looking down, mind you, on Sophie and the guy she's been calling Quack—and her head falls back to follow it up, so her drug-wonder expression disintegrates through distance as the camera gets higher and higher, smoothly—not abruptly—and eventually we see a bird's-eye view of Sophie's whole frame as Quack pulls her up, and we see the unnatural blue of the pool she's lying next to, the pristine white of the concrete around it, and the lawn, and the roof of the villa, and then the fringes of the jungle. And the higher it gets—that is, the farther from her subjective moment the audience physically gets—the more the shot becomes clean and high definition, the more it becomes the stark objective clarity of an aerial view, and the song that was playing in her immediate world, that loving audio colour-swirl, that begins to fade, and pretty soon we're up with the breeze and the grazing wisps of cloud, and we're moving sideways."

"Love it. Very video game. Very Google Earth. I'm all over this visual signature."

"But it's not just style. This is narratively relevant. Once our camera's moving, it's really picking up speed. This isn't, you know, a drift like in the beginning of *The Shining*, this is a rapid drag across the face of the Earth, the jungle blurring in front of the audience. This is a high-speed pull from one location to another, locations over a hundred miles apart, all taking place over about five seconds."

"Five seconds in the right kind of fast-forward can mean a lot of ground covered."

"Exactly. This is a bigtime logistical and physical repositioning for the audience. We're reorienting them in the film's space and time. They need to know precisely where Sophie is, and they need to know in a very visceral sense how far the action is moving. And the bonus with this movement is that, if done clinically enough (and here I *will* enlist some digital help for its implementation) it will give the sense that we are reconnecting with the narrative at exactly the same time we left it. So, we left Sophie at 5.45 p.m., and we're landing with our next thread at 5.45 p.m. You get that?"

"Absolutely." The exec executes his smile-and-point manoeuvre with his index fingers, but keeps the movement contained enough so as not to break the filmmaker's expository rhythm. "So, what's our thread?"

"Our sky-traversing camera starts to slow down once it's breached the jungle, a sort of rapid deceleration that comes to rest over what, from above, looks like a dingy, broken-down conurbation. There's a slummy monsoon poverty that you can see very obviously from this top-down establishing shot, but it's also clear that this poverty is competing with a sort of dirty urbanisation. Think of beige, a pale beige—one infested with rot and splotches of damp and fungus—and then throw electrical wire over the top of it. From above, that's what this city looks like. Live wires over puddles; poisonous snakes. This is the kind of neighbourhood where you might find paedophile sex tourists who've linked their way in through the Deep Web and are making pornography tailored to their tastes in cage sets on the roofs of the buildings."

"That's very specific, Max."

"Well, that's because that's one of the things the camera will see as it lowers its way into the area—in a very cursory, glimpse-like way, of course: it'll pan past it and give it so little focus that the viewer won't really have time to register the horror. They won't fully understand the specifics of what they're seeing. But it's all tonal. Anything goes in this place. And the camera continues down, into the alleyways at street level, and the whole time a new soundtrack is fading in, one that seems to rise out of the street vendors and noise and the chaos of the poverty; the sound is discordant, industrial, a faux-futuristic dystopian drilling that connotes excess and androgyny and body modification."

"I'm sensing a kind of early *Marylin Manson* aesthetic. But a Thai version."

The filmmaker is illustrating the flowing movement of the camera with his arm, sweeping it around corners. "The sound is growing, and as the camera floats in we get our boys in shot. They've pulled their bikes up in this alleyway next to Thai graffiti and garbage bags, and the shadows on the walls are cast by bundles of powerlines all looping and dangling around the place, and it lends the atmosphere something both black and serpentine. We watch them move across the alleyway, Jack first, Olly tailing and smiling incongruously. The camera—still without a cut—tracks in behind them, the music loud and now clearly diegetic, clearly coming from the damp interior of this open archway they're heading into. But as they go inside, vanishing into the lightless void, the camera stops and sort of hovers, and we notice the sign on the wall (the right half of the screen). It's written in Thai. Beneath it, an English subtitle appears: *The Duanphen Hotel*." The filmmaker stops to breathe. He interlocks his fingers, flips his hands and pushes his arms out to flex his knuckles. "You still with me?"

"Very much so," says the exec.

"At this point we cut—using the same sound of the slap we used very early on as a call back to the emotional tone of the film at that point—and find ourselves inside and looking at Olly with the same framing as that initial two-shot with Sophie at the beach bar. Except now he's alone. Where Sophie would have been, there's a headshot of Janet Leigh hanging, but it's as faded and dilapidated as the wall itself. We can hear Thai being spoken off screen, and we can hear music—although at much lower volume now. It's just as we begin to see that Olly is looking, well, *odd*, that we cut again—an axial cut—moving to a close-up, and once we're in there we get the picture. We *absolutely* understand."

INT. THE DUANPHEN HOTEL – DUSK

Jack was buying
Jack was buying
Jack was buying beer
—*that much* Olly could tell. He was ordering in Thai from the hotel's subterranean bar, his body blurred like an impression in a steamy mirror. The bartender, who was the only other person in the place, seemed just as amorphous, a shifting smear of colours. Edgeless shapes rather than humans. Olly looked up at the join between the wall and the ceiling: a balm of natural light was oozing in through a high window that must have been at street level. They'd had to descend stairs to get in here, and while that had happened only moments ago, it already seemed like some antique past. He tried to adjust the muscles of his eyes and gaze into the lighted strip and thought he

could see a dog gnawing at a rubbish bag pressed against the glass. He looked back down at the table. There was perspiration on his palms, so he rubbed them against the tabletop to dry them. His jaw felt tight. He began to massage it, sticking his chin out, then pulling it back in, then rubbing his mandible. His eyelids felt clumsy. But what did it matter? Soph would be arriving soon. She wanted him back and she wanted to change, and the satisfaction he felt seemed to be surging through his entire body: he could feel it in his loins, in his shoulders, in his forearms—a pleasant shooting sensation that reminded him of fireworks, the flames vivid and brilliantine in childhood nights.

He didn't even notice Jack sitting back across from him, sliding a beer over, smiling—a smile which he returned. Jack was his mate, his good friend. He wrenched his jaw open and expressed this sentiment. It was something that needed saying and now was the time to say it. Did he say it?

"Looks like we got you here just in time, fella." Jack's voice echoed a little. "Drink up, buckaroo." It was like his words had bright purple edges on them, like they were the sun and he'd been staring too long.

Olly took hold of the bottle and poured it into his mouth. He was amazed he managed to connect the two, that the liquid passed his lips and washed into his throat; and he was amazed at how cool the bottle felt in his hand. All of this made him happy. "When's Soph gettin ere?" He felt like slouching into his seat, his back sliding down the wall behind him like a piece of tomato.

"Soon, mate," Jack was saying. "Soon enough." He tried to sit himself back up. The side of his face felt droopy and his hair was growing wet and slick with his perspiration. It was almost difficult to hear what Jack was saying, as if his voice were coming from another room. "…thing that got me the most was that you never even asked how I knew about the DaisyFuckYou stuff. Fella, the odds I'd just stumbled on her channel randomly are not favourable. Not in the slightest."

"Yeah!" Olly found himself saying. "That's a *real* good point." He was smiling, sliding back down in the seat again, waggling his finger at Jack in an infantile and lethargic way.

"The weird thing is, to start with I felt I was doing you a favour."

"Ya *were*, mate," Olly mouthed, though he wasn't entirely certain words had come out. He lifted his right arm and produced a thumbs-up. His eyebrows felt like they'd lost contact with his face.

"*Watching* that shit. Well, mate, it was clear you were in need of assistance."

"Fanks," Olly was saying. "Fanks, mate." Back and forward his head went, lolling. "I really preciate it." His nodding rhythm was slowly becoming tribal.

"I mean, don't get me wrong. I was lurking on those sites for recruitment purposes. Girls who do webcam stuff, you know–"

"Yeah, yeah, mate." His wobbling, leaning dance had

become rubbery and wet in its purpose; he was charming invisible snakes.

"–frankly that's ideal on your C.V. if you're looking to work high-risk, one-off holiday jobs in South-East Asia. It speaks to the right kind of psychology, if you know what I mean: willing to take a chance, low on traditional Christian moral fibre, probably estranged from any kind of useful family. And *really* narcissistic—which I think is important. You can flatter the narcissistic into anything, which makes them quite easy to control."

Olly's head was slinking back and forward. "Hymmna," he said, wiping his face suddenly in a slack and simian fashion that suggested he was listening but hearing nothing. "Hymmmneya."

"Anyway, so I saw you caught in the background of someone else's life, just being pummelled and degraded, and, I don't know… I just felt at least there was some kind of justice, some moral imperative, in picking Sophie as a candidate. Normally I go for the easy shot, too. Angle for a couple of skippy-looking lesbians or, normally—because, mate, these ones are our bread-and-butter—the heavily tattooed solo-show girl. Just the right blend of personal damage and self-importance. But I made an exception for you, buddy. I worked for you. You were like a sponsor-me child. A project, matey-mooski."

"Ya got ma back!" Olly heard his voice but didn't feel himself attached to it. His eyes were nearly completely closed, light refracting through the dewy prisms of his lashes and dispersing wildly into the caverns of his pupils.

He felt his hair being rubbed and ruffled, Jack's fingers moving through it. He was becoming a house cat, his head nuzzling toward the human hand, wedging itself into it.

"Well, I tried to have it. So, I picked the old Sophinator purely based on the notion I might be able to emancipate you in the process."

Olly found himself chewing 'emancipate,' trying to open his lips around it: "EEE. MAN. SUE. PATE." Beer was being poured into his mouth to facilitate his swallowing of the word.

"Now, I'm loath to blow my own bassoon on this one, but the range of personal skills I employed in recruiting that misanthropic slag-pile dominatrix to cross the globe for danger-cash were just… Well, fuck, Olly! It was some of my best work."

Olly had heard his name and could see Jack smiling at him through a silky iridescence. His spine felt great. His feet felt great. Everything was great. "That's awesome, mate. Jus…" He felt the tide rush out of his brainstem, then rush right back in again.

"But that's another thing, right. Everyone's all like moo moo moo whattaya doing with ya life, why don't you earn some money? And that's the thing on top of the thing, because the pay for this stuff is way better than a legitimate private-sector equivalent. But then that's the thing on top of *all* the things. You've gotta think about job satisfaction. You gotta think about *fun*, Olly."

"Funnnnnnn." Olly let himself roll across the edge of the sound.

"So for me, mate, it's never been about the money."

"Never about the munnn-knee…" Syllables slipping away, dripping from the table, splashing to the floor and seeping into cracks. "M*unnnn*-knee." He looked around the room; it seemed so soft, lost in rainbow vapours. "Where are we?"

"The Duanphen Hotel bar, matey-moo. Drink up." He was being handed his beer, then he was holding it next to his face, trying to read the small print, which looked like alien script that needed to be touched—a whole tactile language desperately requiring exploration. If he could get close enough, he might turn it inside out and find something. "Of course, you were supposed to just get on with your life without her, mate. You understand that? *You* were meant to be the prime benefactor following the departure of the Sophinator 5000." Olly began making gun sounds, slow motion, and miming explosions with his hands; the prisms of refracted light had manufactured a cartoon warzone in his cerebellum. "However, I did not count on your massively irrational behaviour. Instead of enjoying the luxuries of shrimp, sunshine and freedom, you spent the whole time sending her fawning, illiterate messages. It was bad enough having to update her Facebook without having to field your irrational emo drivel as well. Fuckin' told you not to send her any of that."

"I like it ere," Olly said. He lowered his arms and torso onto the table, prostrating himself, his jaw gurning to the point of deformity. "We should stay, yeah." His mind was lying down somewhere light—a field, a stream. Someone was giggling, and the sound carried like a paper plane. Apples were falling from a tree. "You fink I can eat em?"

"Sure thing, matey." Jack watched him nibble at phantoms, opening and closing his mouth the way a fish does, his breathing laborious and theatrical. "Can I ask ya something, matey? Given that we're spilling. Given that, well, we're at the intersection we're at."

Olly rolled his head across the table, droplets of his sweat beading from the tips of his hair. "Yeeaah, mate." He let his cheek cool on the wood, clenched the muscles in his body, then relaxed them.

Jack reached over and allowed a single droplet of Olly's sweat to link with his index finger. He held it up, then tasted it. "*Really*, why'd ya stick to her after she'd beaten and humiliated you. You coulda gone free here?"

Olly shrugged. He was grabbing for apples rolling away in the grass—it was important to grab them before they tumbled down the hill and ruined his picnic. Jack looked down at him sympathetically. "You're just a shit-dumb koala in a tiger enclosure, huh? You don't mean any harm. You mean any harm, Olly?"

Olly shook his head, rubbing it along the tabletop, almost grinding his face into it, flecked spittle caught in his stubble. The action knocked over Jack's beer, which Jack then watched without moving. The bottle was on its side, glugging its contents onto the wood; he watched it roll numbly toward the edge, cusp, fall and then smash against the stone floor.

Olly did not react at all.

"In the end it's all about making positive steps, right? The dynamic and creative process of giving birth to yourself. Vygotsky said we become ourselves through others. I like to think that's accurate. How 'bout you?" Jack sensed the Englishman move slightly, a subtle stir against the table that he took for assent.

When Kwan arrived with her assistant, Jack was sweeping the glass up with a dustpan and brush he'd taken from behind the bar. Dusk had become darkness and the evening lights in the place had come on, though they were only bright enough to create a lounge mood, something undercut by both the Thai pop and the drooling, mumbling body slumped across the main table.

Jack put down the dustpan, and the bartender, understanding her cue, turned off the music and left.

"Phũ bricākh?" Kwan said, coming down the stairs and pointing at Olly. Her suit was sleek and elegant and entirely out of place in the Duanphen dive.

"Nah. Your guy's out back. This is my uncle Frank."

She moved over and looked at Olly, her kitten heels clicking on the floor. She leaned across his inert mass and inspected him, then, holding his upper body tentatively, pressed her ear against his back and listened for his heartbeat. After a few seconds she pulled away, took a pause, then moved his head with her hands, taking his whole skull and turning it so she could see his face and play with his eyes. Olly murmured a little as she thumbed away at his eyelids before placing his head gently back against the table. "He ready for transport?"

"Should be," Jack said. "Dunno. He might wet himself. Definitely not going to solve any of your conundrums."

Kwan smiled at him. He'd always found her very attractive: early forties, sharp, ethically untroubled. Excellent taste in business attire. "I have no conundrums for him to solve," she said.

"You've never seemed like a lady particularly perplexed by anything." Jack watched her signal to her assistant, a large and relatively young Thai in a plain black shirt. "And I mean that as a compliment."

"Why would I take it any other way?"

The assistant moved round and took Olly under the arms and dragged him out of his seat and toward the service elevator. Jack watched, Olly's feet limp and useless as they bumped across the stone. He hadn't realised this one was going to get to him as much as it was getting to him. Fucking koala.

"Just out of interest…" he said, half starting. Kwan looked up. She'd been rifling through her bag. "I know these things are under wraps and all, but can ya give me a hint about where this guy's going?" The assistant was resting Olly's weight against his knees while the lift came down. "Is it going to be worth his weight?—I guess is what I'm asking."

Kwan smiled at him again and handed over a neatly

wrapped package containing the Australian's payment. "You have done another fine job. I am happy to continue using your services whenever the opportunity arises." She took his face in her hands and looked up at it, holding it in a tender and observational fashion; then the lift arrived, she let it go, turned, and joined her assistant and the incapacitated Olly. Moments later they were gone.

INT. HATCHBACK ON THE HIGHWAY – DUSK

Sophie was in the back seat of the green hatchback, Quack in front of her, Fuck-Suck driving. They'd left the jungle and joined the main highway, vegetation falling away, concrete and metal rising into urban light. She looked out the window—the last of the day was burning through industrial gaps, strobing at her. Fuck-Suck was singing along to some Thai song on the radio and it wasn't making her feel good. Her stomach was aching, and she felt woozy. She found herself grabbing and holding her gut, trying to manipulate the jabbing of internal needles. "Canya tell em ta fucken shut it. Fucken pissin me off."

Quack turned to her gently. He could see she was uncomfortable. "I am sorry, Miss Sophie, but he very much enjoy this song. It about a man who suffer pain, but because the pain have meaning, he find it bearable."

"The fuckaya on about? Fucken daffy cunt." She went back to concentrating on her agony.

Fuck-Suck hit the chorus and extended his voice across a whole range of yos and yas.

"I must urge you, Miss Sophie, not to wrestle too much."

"Wat?" She was turning her knuckles against her intestines, treating them like dough as she attempted to knead away the pain.

"It is important that the package not open early."

"But it fucken urts!"

"For the package to rupture would be very bad for you."

She leaned back in the seat and tried to take her mind off it. Fuck-Suck's song came to an end, and for a moment there was a lull. She could hear the drone of the tires on the tarmac. She touched her stomach again, tracing its circumference with her fingertips, and for a moment she pretended the package was a foetus, something beating with the potential for life. Very suddenly she wanted to cry. It came as a wave, her solar plexus constricting involuntarily as the muscles in her face threatened to collapse. With her hand pressed against her mouth, she tried to regain control, but when a new tune drifted over the radio, this time led by an awful maudlin piano riff, she lost it all over again and found herself biting her hand, sinking her teeth through her skin to force back the rush of emotions.

Fuck-Suck was singing again.

"It's justa fucken comedown," she said, at first to herself, then as a realisation. She could taste her own blood. "Quack! I need more medicine. I'm fucken all in pieces ere."

Quack turned to face her again. He was calm and measured, a man for whom poise came naturally. "Certainly, Miss Sophie. What would you like?"

"All-a it. Anyfing. Just gimmie some fucken drugs!"

"Yes, Miss Sophie." He turned and reached into the glove compartment while Fuck-Suck persevered bravely with the high notes. "He very much like this song also." Quack turned back to her with a selection of capsules in his hand. "This one about truth. It say that just because our heart think something is true, that does not make it *really* true."

INT. EXECUTIVE OFFICE – DAY

"So with her shovelling drugs into her face and swearing at this guy and his cryptic pop-kōans, the camera pulls back, reversing through the window of the car." The filmmaker holds up his left hand, pinches at the palm with his right, then draws it away to illustrate the flow of his conceptual camera. "It's a Hitchcock shot, you know. So now it's outside and looking at the hatchback and speeding along the highway with all the other traffic, and we can feel the sense of velocity and the night air and the yellow and orange lights, and this high-speed camera pans and we can see the scorched silhouette of a city, and the sky has that kind of post-dusk lava tinge that symbolizes–"

The filmmaker is interrupted by the buzzing of the intercom. "Sorry, Max." The exec pushes the button to speak. "Yes, Benny?"

"I have your dog for you, sir."

"Excellent. That's great. Could you bring it in?"

"Right away, sir."

The exec lets go of the button and looks at the filmmaker. "Guy certainly earns his keep."

There is a moment of silence in which the rain can be heard against the window, then the door opens and a fully grown bullmastiff sniffs its way into the room, followed by Benny, who is holding it by a lead. The filmmaker turns in his chair to look, while the exec leaves his seat entirely, rounding the desk to greet the dog. He kneels down next to it and rubs its head and says, "Hello, boy. Hello there." He looks up at Benny. "Did he come with a name?"

"Henry, sir. Which I feel he suits. He is three years old, fully trained and ready to go. Although he looks like he will make a good guard dog based simply on size, he is, in fact, quite docile. Bullmastiffs, while very friendly, are known to be quite lazy dogs. They–"

"Thanks, Benny," the exec says, getting to his feet and taking the lead. "I don't need the tasting notes."

"Will that be all, sir?"

"Yes, pal." The exec strokes the dog's coat. "Take the rest of the day off."

"Thank you, sir."

Benny leaves and the exec unclips the lead and lets the dog pad around the office. It decides to sniff the filmmaker with its dark snout and lick at his hand; the filmmaker is mildly repulsed and wipes away the residual saliva on the hem of his jacket. The dog's face is floppy and its eyes are vulnerable. It appears to be content with its surroundings. "Not a dog person?" the exec asks, sitting back into his Portuguese chair.

"No, it's not that. I don't know… Where were we?"

EXT. MOUNTAIN ROADS – NIGHT

It was fully dark by the time Jack was riding back to the resort through jungled hills and feeling narcotically lightheaded, the beam of his moped casting a grainy yellow triangle into a night that seemed to hold more terrors than usual. Still, there was nothing to do but swerve into them. Hunt them. Chase them into the darkness and feast. He drifted back and forward across the lanes, flirting with the death instinct and asking it to dance.

After Kwan had departed he'd lingered in the hotel bar awhile, drinking beer he didn't need to drink and chatting with the bartender in Thai. It was important that he leave space between Kwan's departure and his own, but even if he hadn't needed to, he would have stayed. He sat at the bar itself rather than the table, although he kept glancing back at it, half imagining a chalk outline of Olly's body in its slumped and ultimate posture. The bartender had noticed this and asked Jack about it in a not unfriendly or invasive way. They'd met before, of course—like him, she was one of the many confidential nodes essential to illegal efficacy, reading from the same sinful hymnbook he was and singing in basically the same Hell choir, so her manner of query was professional in nature, laced with a kind of workplace curiosity. What was up? Who was the guy? Paedophilic sex tourist? Serial rapist? Some financial monster who'd Ponzied the feebleminded out of their savings? Because Jack certainly didn't have the same post-deal ebullience he usually had, no jokes about penguins wearing sunglasses or giraffes trying on shorts. Instead he was mildly sullen and discoursing monotonously about psychologists.

He looked at the bartender, cleared his throat: "Get this: Endel Tulving—born in Estonia, of all places—he said that *memory is a bend in time's arrow*, which is a needlessly convoluted albeit poetic way of saying that remembering things is like time travel. Apparently only humans can do that. We're the only species that make that temporal jump. Apparently."

The bartender took the hint and decided she was overstepping. What business was it of hers anyway? Obviously it was something bad. In this industry, sometimes it was better not to know. She turned and fiddled with her phone and so only partially caught what he said next. Something about suicide.

She found herself looking back. "Suicide?"

But then it was all in English.

"Nah, nah—a suicide *booth*. Somewhere you can nip into if you want to check out. Ping. Pop. Frizzle. My idea wasn't the booth, it was the *switch*. I had an idea for a broken switch. Or it would *seem* broken. So, you go in, think, 'I wanna die 'cause my toast is burnt,' then ya slam the big black death button with the skull on it. But it doesn't work. Not the first time, anyway. Or the second or the third. The thing would only work if you hit it ten seconds apart, idea being you'd sort the dilettantes from the dedicated. It would only allow the decision if there were a sustained and wholehearted commitment to it. Anyway, I like my switch idea, and if you can knit that into the fabric of reality and make it a widget, matey-moo… shit, I'll buy it."

"Khuṇ s̄bāy dī h̄ịm?" The bartender looked concerned.

"Sorry," he said, this time in Thai. "I'm fine. No worries." He finished his drink and smiled, reëstablishing his decorum.

In the open street outside the bar he stood beside the two mopeds. Dusk had closed. It wasn't Jack's usual style (typically he liked to keep his head as sharp as he could keep it) but he'd decided a shaved bump was a good idea—something to create a remove from himself. He extracted one of the techno-green pills from his wallet and nibbled an edge off, chiselling a rough third away with his front teeth and letting the chemical horror dissolve in his saliva. He could hear someone screaming in the distance, though the echoes made it impossible to tell which direction it was coming from, the treble of the local tongue rendering it both genderless and ageless. Just a scream. A guy shuffled past him with a bamboo pole balanced across his shoulders, the ends weighed down with pungent bundles of dead ducks. Despite the fact it hadn't rained for nearly a fortnight, the air felt wet. He rolled the engine over on his bike and picked his way out of town.

What had he forgotten? What was still to tie up before the affair was closed and all links to his existence had either been erased or muddied to the point of unintelligibility. The bartender would return the second moped the following day and no one would care. And Jack would dump the phones in the right places and let the batteries die... Ultimately time was his real friend—no one would care until Olly failed to arrive back in London, and even then there would be a substantial grace period, a leeway for the impulsivity of youth. And after that...? Well, what was the general capacity for caring about the Ollys of the universe? What was the public's investigatory interest? Was he even worth a short news item? Unless there was genuine sympathy, there wasn't a story. Stories were for school kids with whole lives ahead of them, or scholars, or revered members of a community. And Olly wasn't a sportsman or a celebrity or someone with money. Because there was a socio-economic truth in all this: each life has an objective economic value measured via a calculation of net worth, public interest and potential, and no matter how one tweaked the figures, the Englishman came in with a low score. Olly, as a whole, was not worth more than the sum of his parts. And every day that passed with no one caring would be one more day in which the evidentiary trail was smeared and contaminated, spoiled irreversibly. High turnover is tourism. Fingerprints and DNA are eliminated by housekeeping inside twenty-four hours. Good luck finding anything in a month.

Jack was coming up hard as he sped into the hills, the grazing of the drugs slicing through the sludge of the beer, but also somehow taking him sideways, displacing his consciousness. As he leaned into dark corners and churned the accelerator, he felt himself watching himself, hovering above his body and looking down on it, riding a third-person perspective. And then his mind began to drift, across psychologists that spoke of the unconscious, across Jungian archetypes and Skinnerian rat boxes and postconventional stages of moral development. He was in a hot sea, floating, looking up at an eclipsed sun and contemplating the significance of celestial alignment. Random. Coincidental. Light and dark and pulsing wavelengths where amplitude was only meaningful in that it existed: one plus negative one equals the collective dream.

INT. INDETERMINATE – MORNING

Olly woke with little memory of where he'd been or what was going on, and for quite a few seconds he didn't move. Partly this was because he was comfortable. His body felt like it was supposed to be where it was, half wrapped in a sheet and satisfied with the state of its lethargy, and for a fleeting moment he thought he was in England, in his bed in his South London flat. Soon he would have to rise and have breakfast and prepare for a day at work where he would haul cinderblock and pour foundation.

But the ambience was wrong for London. He could sense the ocean's presence—the salty insistence, the low hum of its immensity: a natural aesthetic counterpoint to the metal grind of South Circular traffic. This wasn't Peckham. And the longer he looked at the ceiling the more he could differentiate the subtle shapes of the light on the paint—tropical light—and it came back to him that he was on holiday, that he was in Thailand, that he was at a resort. Tetris blocks fell into place.

He showered, standing under the hot stream and letting his mind paddle through its own darkness. He didn't recall getting back to the resort. The last thing he really remembered was…? Mopeds. He could remember leaving with Jack and riding the coast, jungle glades and sea views.

The *tiger*.

Like orange lightning he recalled the impressive smell of the animal as it reared on its hind legs and tried to open him up, claws out, the growl that seemed to gouge some essential part of the world. A growl that tore and ripped. Had he looked into its eyes long and hard? Had he seen something primal and pure? It all seemed like Voodoo: a dance with burned spirits, a black spell from Mother Underworld.

Out of the shower and still dripping, he looked for his phone without success. Nor, for that matter, could he find his suitcase or any of his things. It was as if the place had been cleaned out in his absence.

He sat outside his cabin and let dawn light warm his face. It was obvious he'd been on a bender—otherwise he would have remembered how he'd got home. Yet, physically, he felt surprisingly good. His body felt strong, his muscles full. His mind, on the other hand, was staccato—like something had jammed itself in there and messed around with the circuits.

He watched the clouds.

A sudden memory of apples, of a picnic under a tree where the apples dropped from above and he'd had to collect them. He couldn't tell if this was real or imagined, whether he'd been there alone or with other people. He attempted to channel his mind toward that single memory, to clear the fog from its edges, but it remained resolutely vague. And how long had the phone been ringing in the cabin, its sound surfacing as if from the bottom of a lake—a signal from someone else's life, an elongated peal that, now that he was aware of it, felt like an aural circular saw, a high-speed grating of steel on steel.

He moved in and picked it up. The ringing stopped, but he felt he could still hear it, trace amounts caught echoing inside the geometry of his skull. "Yeah?"

"Guess who, matey-moo?"

There was an instant wave of relief. "Mate, wat appened?"

"All kinds of things, sunshine. It's all happening." Jack's voice seemed paradoxically intimate and distant; Olly felt he was being whispered to from the far side of a hall, the whisper itself arriving with static clarity.

"Wat's appenin? Wad we do las night?" He rubbed his face with the palm of his hand. "I aint remember nuffink."

"You, matey-moo! Sophie. The whole koala-balloon. Mate: You. Were. A. Monster. Always are."

"Yeah, but wad we get up ta?"

"Look, fella: postmeridian, it was a rough trip to Drunksville. An expedition, and you told me a whole load of bullshit about your feelings and ended up eating quite a portion of your own shit."

"Wat appened ta Soph?"

"You're a case study, mate. You're a fucking wombat."

Olly found himself squeezing the bridge of his nose. "Mate—Sophie. Wat appened?"

"She's out on the beach, fella. Think she's planning on a swim to that island. Might wanna catch her before–"

Olly didn't wait around for the rest. He was out the door of the cabin and making his way across the grass toward the beachfront, almost scrambling. Against laboured breaths he looked up and down the coast, and it took him a period of adjustment to realise that the beach itself was empty. The sun was extremely low. It was still too early for people.

He stood for a moment and wondered whether he was still drunk—or drugged. He couldn't remember what he'd taken, and his brain felt like it was struggling to make it back to the shallow end of the pool. He looked down the beach again, squinting, first south, then north, then wading right out into the water until he was waist deep in order to get a full view of the convex coast.

And there she was.

She was waving to him. It had to be her. She was a fair distance down the beach, but he could tell her walk and the shape of her body even when she was only an outline, a silhouette—less than the height of his thumbnail with his arm outstretched. He waved.

She waved back.

She was dragging something. Rolling it. And as he looked closer he could see that it was a suitcase, its plastic arm fully extended as she trailed it behind her. Like an airhostess, he thought. Like a woman who'd circumnavigated the globe and was coming back to him. And standing there in the water he felt momentarily sublime, his chest warming from within and spreading outward through is body. She was coming. It was finally happening.

He started wading in, looking out at her. He would meet her halfway. And as he came up upon the beach and began to stride, he could make out her dress—the violet one, strapless, her shoulders cool and lithe—and the high heels that she seemed to be navigating over the sand with genuine control (so *her*!) the flowing hair that he had let fall against his face countless times. Why restrain himself? Why play this cool? And then he was running to her and she was growing, becoming fully realised. And she was smiling—a symbol of reconciliation and affection and love. This was his girl in a sparkling dress during a golden dawn, and he knew he wanted a picture—that this was the one he would want forever.

"I'm sorry!" he gushed, almost spraying the sand as he pulled up to her; he leaned down to her and kissed her, took her face in his hands and held his lips to hers. "I'm sorry fa everyfink." He found her eyes, her head angled up, and made certain she knew what he felt, that what he said was truth. "I love ya, baby. *Sophie*. I love ya." And she smiled back up at him to return this ardour, to show that everything was okay and that love was not only reciprocal but entwined in everything, cellular—that there would never be fights again: only the sweet embrace of human perfection, of each other.

With this placid grin of affirmation she lifted a hand to his face and cupped his cheek, caressed his mouth. Be still, the gesture said. Be calm. I have something to show you, and with her eyes locked on his she pulled back and held up a finger to instruct that he wait. She knelt down in the sand next to her suitcase and began to unzip it, the light of the low sun glinting from the myriad panels of her dress. "Whatcha got, Soph?" he found himself saying, and he followed her artful and utterly mesmerising hand as it drew along the perimeter of the case: the bottom, along the side, across the top. And then she opened it like an assistant to a gameshow host, smoothly revealing what was behind door number three.

Olly had to look closer.

The inside was dark and wet and shiny—a meat pile, glossy with the juices of its own freshness. "We avin a BBQ or somefin?"

Sophie smiled back at him. "No, Olly," she said. "We aint. This is all yours."

"Eh?"

"Look at yourself, Olly."

His chest was open. The skin had been pulled back,

his ribcage prised apart like cupboard doors. He could see his own spinal column, a hollowed out cavern where his torso should have been. He tried to breathe, but his lungs were in the suitcase, expanding and contracting atop a pile of his other organs. He wanted to shudder and weep, but his nervous system was malfunctioning.

There was a rupture somewhere, something popping—the sudden warm flow of aneurystic blood across his frontal lobe. One of his eyes closed. There was scratching at his retina. Sophie was holding a piece of his insides—a kidney, his liver?—and he could feel his heart beating against the nylon interior of the case.

He was on his back and floating.

It was impossible to say how he'd got there, how he'd moved from the beach to this log-like posture in the sea. But he could feel things inside him, moving and tugging at essential parts, and he would have coughed and spluttered as the water washed into his throat except that he was no longer taking air—the salinity simply splashed in and swilled about—and when he managed to angle his vision, to tweak his lethargic eyeballs away from the lucidity of the blue sky, he could see Sophie, sitting in the hollow of his torso, looking ahead, paddling with her hands. He had become her canoe, water sluicing around his skull as she propelled them forward.

An echo in the drainpipe of his ears; liquid spilling into gutters. Rats scurrying across sourceless shafts of light, squeaking. Sloshing. He felt so light and so hot. It did not matter that he could not breathe, that moment to moment his movement stiffened and his sensations eroded, that he could no longer taste the salt or feel the weight of Sophie moving on his spine, or see her. Or even feel hot. Or feel light.

And it pulled apart, like spiderweb interrupted.

And this was Olly's final dream.

And as his brain began to die the dream itself started to degrade, its internal integrity dissolving, its structure coming loose—fragments of a man as a grotesque human raft propelled by an absent obsession. Taking on water. Apples in the ocean. Babies giggling in the mist. And all of this was frittering away mathematically—parabolically—until, little by little, bit by bit, there was nothing at all.

INT. EXECUTIVE OFFICE – DAY

"Wait," says the exec, halting the filmmaker in the flow of his exposition. "So, is Olly dead or what? Is that the last we're going to see of him in the story?"

The filmmaker drops his hands, which had been mid-gesture attempting to convey the evanescence of a spirit into the fabric of the universe. He is irritated by the break in his rhythm. "What do *you* think?" He can't help but tilt his head slightly to the side, and it gives him the look of a teenager annoyed by the fact his parents don't understand him.

"I think he's dead. Although I've gotta say, it's not all that clear." The exec leans down and rubs the bullmastiff behind the ears. The dog enjoys this.

"Look, a level of ambiguity is important if you want to get right into the recesses of the experience itself. But yes, he's dead. By the end of this scene he's completely and totally dead."

"Well how is that any kind of ending for him?"

"It's *not* the ending for him."

"What, so he's coming back? Like in a flashback? A dream sequence?" The exec leaves the dog and sits up straight again, looking across at the filmmaker. "If he wakes up and it's all been a dream, then–"

"Jesus Christ! Give me some credit."

The exec lifts his palms in a gesture of defence. "Sorry. You know how it is. People can get pretty myopic inside a fit of creative passion."

The filmmaker produces a flatulent dismissive sound with his lips to indicate his contempt at the exec's assumption. "I know I've got a few hack qualities, but I'm not a fucking ten-year-old. All a dream. Please."

"I said I was sorry."

There is a sudden silence between them and the exec again becomes aware of the rain against the window. For a change, he feels unnaturally present in his own life. The filmmaker, on the other hand, is quite rapidly lost in thought, his gaze unfocused and cast toward the corner of the office. When the exec speaks again, it takes the filmmaker a moment to register and remove himself from his private hypnosis.

"So what happens next?"

The filmmaker sucks in a breath, but this time when he starts speaking his hands remain planted in his lap and he does not look directly at the exec. "Our frame skirts the edges of the tangible and the intangible. It unwinds itself across a temporal district that is simultaneously expanding and contracting; shadows will gain substance while all that is concrete will crumble into wraithlike formlessness."

"You might be losing your audience with this, Max."

"We pan upwards and find ourselves looking directly at the sun. Only, it is a blackened sun, flaming apocalyptically along its circumference. The mood is cosmic and elemental."

INT/EXT. ABSTRACT SPACE – SOLAR ECLIPSE

There are equations for everything, inside every instant, even if—with the limits of our language and our insufficient tools for measurement and calculation—we don't really have the capability to formulate them. How much did Olly suffer? Could that be marked onto a chart in some way? Could an objective number be produced which considered the intensity of both his physical and psychological trauma when offset against his sensitivity to it? Because if that could be done, then it could be graded and ranked, cross-referenced against his overall existential worth, and measured against the suffering of others. He could be given a value—a raw number—and we would then know for sure if his torture and misery could be justified. Certainly Kwan's customers, had they known (had they been *able* to know) would have thought it justified. The fact they were using her service in the first place meant they were a certain type of person, typically high on the belief in their own exceptionalism and happy to ignore anecdotes and empathy in favour of numbers.

Either way, in all cases the customers remained ignorant of the human source of their salvation and the particulars of what had taken place behind the scenes. This remains one of the benefits of personal wealth and fully integrated global capitalism: everything is for sale, there's a market, a black market, and—in Thailand's case—a *red* market, and if you have the cash and the savvy, you can get whatever you need without guilt. Because who was going to ask questions? Lee Yakubu certainly wasn't. As the director of a large Japanese fishing concern, he'd made tough choices right through his career, stoically axing whole divisions of workers and medicating himself through physical pain to execute working hours regular people would've seen as inhuman. At fifty-five this was about to cost him his kidney, but it was also buying him a new one. Who it came from was not something he was worried about. Speed and efficiency were all that mattered.

It was a similar story for Mikahail Vasiliev, the forty-three-year-old son of a Russian oligarch and the unfortunate victim of spare time and easy money. Years of heavy drinking and an addiction to Vicodin meant he too was in need of a quick kidney; but, as a man of means and a man of connections, he was not in the habit of waiting. And it was especially important to him because his own father was no longer in peak condition. It was time to step up and set things right; he would have to take over the management of their various business interests, attend social functions in a more upstanding capacity, and leave behind all the churlish trimmings of his spoiled and hyper-extended youth. New levels of behavioural discretion were called for, even a total personal change. As his father said to him most recently—albeit in Russian—"Instead of beating bitches up, how about you marry one of them." The kidney would be Mikahail's new beginning.

For Philippe Lamarque it was less about starting over than it was about extending the end, squeezing out another few years of good ratings and high levels of public esteem. As a long-serving Argentinian T.V. personality he'd enjoyed a relatively illustrious career in his home nation, moving seamlessly between the assorted roles of the modern televisual celebrity (gameshow host, travel show host, venerated celebrity panellist) and he'd become very used to lingering in the wider VIP lounge of life: a man for whom the velvet rope was always pulled aside and for whom a favour was always granted; a man who'd ultimately substituted family and close relationships for the quick sex and sugary trappings of fame. Except, at sixty-three, while he was still right at the top of all the most important guest lists, he was nowhere near the top of any transplant lists. Frankly, the thing with his pancreas was a massive affront, and he took the affliction extremely personally (it was like the paparazzi had jumped his fence, shat in his pool, then invaded his body) and he found it virtually impossible to conceive of an existence in which he was not at high-functioning fettle and being recognised by strangers while eating in stylish restaurants. No. There was no way he was going down in such ignominious fashion, not because of something as ugly and pointless as a pancreas (What did a pancreas even do?!). So damn the illegality, he was buying a new one.

And the harvest continued.

The proud new owner of Olly's flexible athletic liver was a South Korean tech tycoon named Park Moo-Chan. Moo-Chan actually knew what human flesh tasted like and how much it cost per pound. Olly's would be his third liver—purchased for transplant, not to eat—and with the speed and efficiency of the delivery service Moo-Chan was beginning to believe that he might be able to live forever. Why not? Immortality existed right there in the interstice between perpetually improving science and his own personal fortune. And he'd always been a proponent of surgery of every kind, whether aesthetically motivated (like his many tucks and lifts) or actually essential to the maintenance of life. Oftentimes he dreamed of the awesome patchwork fusion he might become, a consciousness floating in the fleshy life raft of all new parts, an *ultra*modern Prometheus free of a father complex, eventually supplemented (he dared to believe) by such add-ons and mod cons as titanium fingers, digital vision, and an adamantium skull. What a horrendous and beautiful machine he would be. But if the inevitable happened before science could catch up and his body was assailed, for example, by some stealthy and malignant tumour, then he had a plan. Cryogenics was improving day-by-day, and his wealth was helping to fund it. If he were truly forced to kick off the coil, then straight into cryo-sleep he would go until a solution could be found. And it was for these reasons that Park Moo-Chan walked without fear. He wore the bullish gleam of invincibility. He commanded shareholders and boardrooms as if they were insects and had the steely aura of a demigod. Of all the recipients of Olly's bits, he was the only one to fly in his own medical team to seize the organ he needed before having the operation performed elsewhere.

Yet not all the benefactors of Olly's body bonanza were titans of ego and industry. George and Mary Porter simply wanted to save their chess-prodigy son Hugo. All signs were that he could be a genuine contender in the junior division at the FIDE World Championships, but he would need a new heart to do so. They weren't overtly bad or unethical people, just middle class Scottish lawyers who'd exhausted all their other options. It was on an evening after George had watched Hugo beat a visiting Grand Master by utilising a technique that would've unnerved Bobby Fischer that he *knew* he had to do more. Hugo had looked so pallid and grey as he'd moved his pawns, hunched into his chair at the club and wrapped in a blanket in a way that made is father think of polio and senility and gerontic decay, but not his son! Not a fourteen-year-old boy! So it was that under the cover of night and with a proxy IP address George began his wary foray through the Dark Web, inching anxiously into the shadowy corners of the organ trade, the family's combined savings converted to cryptocurrency and ready to purchase any kind of hope. Once he'd found a contact that seemed legitimate he shared the information with his wife, then they'd talked with Hugo—who, with his analytical brain, could sift realistically through the potential risks—and then they'd all agreed to give it a shot.

And it had worked.

Two months later Hugo was wheeled out of a shady Thai medical centre with a scar and a strong new ticker, determined to checkmate the world.

And that was that. Other than his left eyeball, which Kwan kept in a sleek looking jar in a special room along with many other eyeballs, the rest of the Englishman was rolled into the fire and burned away. No need for his corneas or his lungs. No demand for his spleen. No market at all for his cold paperweight of a brain.

In the years to come very few people would ever think of Olly. Even his parents, who had been long and acrimoniously divorced, were rarely conscious of him, each phlegmatically assuming he was probably in contact with the other. His construction job was filled quickly. The room in his flat was occupied. He left no hole inside a social circle that had been tenuous and accidental in the first place (*Seen Olly recently? Nah, mate. Oi, football's on!*).

Yet while he was most certainly forgotten, he was no longer entirely meaningless. Sure, his pointless fleet as an organised collection of atoms was over—his haircut was gone, and no one would ever again hear his voice in person or sit to have beers with him; but in some small yet arguably crucial way, in death he became more significant and personally virulent than ever. Because despite his happy donors' desires to blank out the source of their extended longevity, something both gross and incontrovertible happened to each one of them—generally small changes at first, yes, but ones that grew over time as their biologies fully bonded with their new slice of working class British meat. For Lee Yakubu—the director of the Osaka fishing concern—his ability to concentrate in the months following his kidney transplant grew steadily worse. At first his lapses occurred only with paperwork, late at night when his eyes dragged themselves across the edges of contractual Kanji; then it was during the day, in the middle of meetings and phone calls (he would just lose the thread); finally it was virtually all the time, his colleagues suggesting, barely out of ear shot, that some malicious and degenerative disease had not only taken over Yakubu's brain, but had started murdering the hostages as well.

For Mikahail Vasiliev, the operation really had signalled a new beginning, and while many of his cohorts blamed his shift in temperament on the sudden death of his father, that didn't make a lot of sense. To run Russian corporate interests successfully, a leader must be iron-fisted, hard-headed and, to a certain extent, arrogantly disagreeable—all of which Vasiliev had been, only with the added inconveniences of also being profligate, hedonistic and prone to sexual violence. In the aftermath of the operation, however, his tastes began to change. Quite literal tastes, too, as he developed an inexplicable affinity for salted peanuts and warm ale, as well as a bizarre emotional connection to the fortunes of second division football team Millwall United. But it was in the sex club that his cronies really noticed something was wrong—again misascribing the change to some (hopefully temporary) post-dad empathy wave—when Vasiliev wasn't turned on by the prospect of suspending prostitutes in chains and ropes and treating them to mild electric shocks. His heart just wasn't in it. And without enthusiasm or an erection, it was difficult for anyone else in his gang to enjoy it either—so goes the Mutually Motivated Erection Theory of sadistic gangbangs and orgies. So they stopped doing it. Then Vasiliev married a woman who told him what to do all the time. However, with his new levels of agreeableness, he'd developed the life-habit of letting *everyone* tell him what to do, so much so that by the time his new kidney began to fail ten years down the road he had neither the money nor the connections to acquire another one.

As for Philippe Lamarque, the Argentine celebrity, although his body regained the ability to produce insulin, within a year of the operation he had almost entirely lost his charisma, not to mention his patented verbal quickness. Where snarky sarcastic responses had been the man's calling card (who could forget Lamarque's withering rejoinders on Channel 3's flagship panel show *Idiota de la*

Semana) he was now soft and vulnerable, often out of his depth, a target so easy for the other panelists that before long they simply didn't bother, unwilling to seem cruel in the face of obvious weakness. And one thing followed another, as is the way in industries as ruthless and mercenary as entertainment media: soon there were no more easy travel shows to host, no cushy game shows; then no invites to functions or gallery openings or award ceremonies, his name slipping farther and farther down the guest lists until, eventually, it failed to appear at all.

Unfortunately, it was a similar story for Hugo Porter and his capacity for chess. His parents had been reluctant to put any pressure on him at first—the boy had had the organ of all organs swapped out after all and deserved a little recovery leeway—but as the qualifying round for the FIDA World Champs approached Hugo seemed to be actively getting worse. Initially the mistakes were forgivable, the product of lapses in concentration; then they were glaring; and then, quite abruptly, it was like he'd forgotten the rules altogether (*Dad, how's the knight move again?*). But the Porters took this blow in their stride. They were deeply in debt after the operation, but no level of financial trouble or loss of talent in their son could be balanced against the sheer fact of his continuing to live. And Hugo had changed in other ways, too—positive ones, if viewed with the right kind of relaxed eyes. He was simpler and happier now, toting an earnest goodwill that was rare in the Porter bloodline, but, given the strain they'd all gone through, extremely welcome—the synthesis of Olly's more koala-bear qualities diluting the inherently highly-strung genes of Scottish lawyers. And maybe it was this strange union that allowed Olly's heart to keep working inside Hugo's body. To keep going. To keep pumping blood vigorously and vitally for years and years beyond its expected term. And that's something.

And, of course, there was Park Moo-Chan, the part-time cannibal and tech tycoon who'd planned to live forever. Having had his new liver flown direct to his own private and highly-skilled medical team in South Korea, Moo-Chan went under the knife, then flatlined right there on the operating table. In the commotion that followed—the kind that occurs when any important person expires suddenly and the resulting blame frenzy induces temporary insanity—his team completely forgot about the post-mortem cryogenic protocol and left his body to stiffen beyond salvage on a gurney. Whether Olly can be credited for any of that is a matter for metaphysical debate.

INT. AIRPORT SECURITY GATE – NIGHT

The lights in the terminal were pulsing and Sophie's left hand felt soaking wet and like it didn't belong to her. She was holding her passport, pinched between thumb and forefinger, and staring at the whole hand-&-document tableau. It seemed separate from everything else—outlined and in focus against the grey airport carpet and hanging significantly. She looked left, though she didn't know why. Her vision was fuzzy. She tried to lick her upper lip, but her tongue felt rubbery and desiccated and didn't seem to have the necessary elasticity to do what she wanted it to. She made a grunting sound and sensed that her eyelids were closing in a way that was problematic.

Where was she?

She kept finding herself unmoored from her task and

was having enormous difficulty staying connected to any basic sequence of events. For reasons she couldn't fathom she pictured pine logs fluming into a North American river, then tissue paper being pulled from a tissue box, then jungle views as howler monkeys filled the empty spaces, simian grins staring back at her from the darkening gaps between branches. Momentarily she was aware that she had a responsibility to fulfil

—she had somewhere to be or somewhere to get—

but as soon as she found this thread she seemed to catch another one and track off again into insular engrossment that probably, if she could just grasp it all for a second, didn't look good from the outside.

Where the fuck was Quack?

Or Fuck-Suck?

Something was tapping on her right shoulder and she turned to meet it and found a short Thai man with parted hair and a polo shirt smiling back at her, his face near and then far and then near and then far, and he was opening and closing his mouth and she could see his teeth *so* clearly. His teeth were bright and straight and bold. She was agreeing with him, nodding up and down, and up and down, her neck elastic and pendulous, and it was only after he'd faded out of view, back into the yellow fur beyond her chemically-shortened field of vision, that she realised this guy had been trying to return her carry-on luggage, that she'd unwittingly dropped the little carry-on case and walked away from it and gone into some kind of private hole, that she was staring at her passport in the middle of the security area and was sweating and gurning like a creature from a swamp.

Fucken concentrate ya daffy cunt.

It was difficult to sort what was in her head and what wasn't.

Daffy cunt! Daffy cunt!

Half-an-hour earlier she'd been in the back seat of the hatchback. Fuck-Suck had been singing and her gut had felt like it was being hollowed out with rusty knives. Quack had turned and fed her pills—green ones and blue ones and red ones—and then the pain had started to recede, drifting into some shadowy corridor, fading back bit by bit until she couldn't recall it, couldn't even summon the vestigial sense of it... Fuck-Suck was singing again—though this time his body was giving off light and warmth; and Quack was explaining the lyrics again in that same steady butler's voice that was now also the loving voice of a benevolent and eternal god: *this one about how a lover cannot be hurt without first giving permission, but I think this is not so true.*

Then the car was parked and she was smoking cigarette after cigarette in the darkness, ashing from the window while she told Quack things she felt she needed to say, given that their time was coming to an end, given all that he'd done for her.

Quack had stopped her though

—*there is not time, Miss Sophie, for sentimentality*—

and he'd reminded her of her obligations and given her a piece of carry-on luggage and together they had gone through the instructions again.

Step 1. Step 2. Step 3.

And remember not to wrestle too much; for the package to open early would be very bad for you.

Step 1. Step 2. Step 3.

The car was gone and she was standing alone in the satin darkness on the shoulder of the road clutching the extendable handle and wearing her heels and still obliterating cigarettes, massacring them, and her task: Step 1: walk across the grass and through the car park toward the light of the International Departures Terminal.

Waves of goodwill rushed through her body, chemicals propelling her spirit of adventure and personal success. She dragged hard on her smoke and it felt like she'd managed to burn the whole thing down in one inhalation and wanted more. And *fuck this was amazing.* Here she was in her dress in the dark, dragging her little wheelie case into a foreign airport all lit up like some burning wonderland, and she was *eating* this thing: *killing* it. She'd reached her personal zenith: fuck all the losers in London: this was *her* moment: and she wanted to take her phone out and grab a selfie, the flash lighting up the night and her face like hot truth but doing nothing to diminish the blast zone of her pupils, Terminal Four a golden bouquet over her shoulder…

Except she had no phone.

How long had she been patting herself down in the darkened rows of Long Term Parking, looking for a non-existent cell in non-existent pockets? She straightened herself to collect her bearings and smoke yet another cigarette and feel the silky persistence of the night air.

Her heels sounded like someone else's and she found herself turning circles, trying to catch whoever it was that was clipping and clopping behind her like some dance-party horse.

';[;][l]kkjk#;#,.[l
[]]][::;#[]

→ She closed her eyes, but the inside of her lids defied the darkness. All she could see was bright white light.

She stood still.

I's jus waitin 'er at the minute, finking like…finking. Jeknow wat I mean?

And in this swirling turbulence on the edge of the airport's carpark she somehow managed a thought about her absentee father—who'd liked to touch her, certainly—and she felt now this was in some way relevant to other things in her life, like muzzles and violence ###########; and she managed a thought about her mother—drunk unemployed *slag*—all of it connecting in the astral flow of things and aligning. Because she was better than that, but in the grand concatenated link of the universe it had all brought her here:

Jeknow wat I mean?

Except, she kept forgetting she had something to do. Somewhere to *be*.

Step 1.

Step 1: walk across the grass, the car park, the light…

Find direction. Forge ahead.

So she did, the drone of plastic wheels against concrete vibrating lattices on the rear of her skull and seeming to grow louder—louder and louder as she moved inexorably toward the throbbing incandescent fun park of the International Departures Terminal.

Then blur.

Then she'd been holding her passport and staring at the grey floor.

Howler monkeys in the jungle.

Daffy cunt! Daffy cunt!

She was drinking warm water from a faucet in the airport bathroom. Melting. Her body operating via instinct and rote response, her mind malfunctioning badly.

Time. Steps. Purpose.

People were coming and going all around her in spiked clanks and echoes within echoes, taps shutting off and on as water hissed and splashed in basins and Dyson Airblades whirred like jet engines threatening to burn her brain to puree. Light scattered and blitzed in wild florescent dances, sparking cruelly in the corners of her vision and threatening to ignite the whole room, to blow the building into craters and bent metal. The overstimulation was monumental. She had to stare at herself in the mirror concertedly—violently—in order to regain her bearings.

What bearings?

She removed her sunglasses—how long had they been on?

Her face didn't seem to belong to her. Step 2.
Step 2.
Her left eyeBall was filling up with blood.
Wait.
She put her sunglasses back on.
Step 2: Go through security.

She had to move—not least because of what she was seeing in the reflection. Although she couldn't really be sure of the truth of any of it now, because all that laughter almost certainly had to be in her own head, and there was no way the wall tiles were really mapped with a tentacular nightmare of veins and arteries, a moist red network spreading from the toilet doors and across the floor and growing thicKer and thicker the more she looked at it. No. Way. And yet it still bothered her that it might all climb to the ceiling and enter the vents—because what if it clogged the air conditioning? What then?

She felt superheated, choked by the constriction of her dress and its tight pull around her breasts and ribs. Internal flames. Straightjackets. TweeZers removing whole zones of humAn skin and a furnace scorching her lungs.

Back to the mirror to lift her glasses: the white of her left eye the colour of a coKe can.

Leave the bathroom!

She turned and tripped over her carry-on case, but the movement itself was good. It was conclusive. Motion was what would save her. Stasis would spell doom. To stand still would be to cYcle into another hole and be stuck there foreVer.

She collected her case, felt the plastic handle in the certainty of her damp palm, then clattered her way back into the maelstrom of the teRminal.

→ Reverberating moments inside moments and glass tornados shattering, re-forming, shAttering again. Delays and departures, volatile passenger messages, hostile reminders, lost warNings. Cancelations. Flights 4 [5] 6 through 1 2 [3] boarding now at all gates, no gates, gates now closing. No Smoking & No Screaming! {{}]}}{{ Thai instructions leaKing in Satanic walkie-talkie crackles;;;;;;[;digital boards crumbling in endless dysleXic hailstorms; off-planEt interstellar advertising: lingerie, perfume—glowing FLESH piXels, motorised death carts, howler monkeys: hostesses with raZor pillboX hats and ceramic smiles: *now burning luggage for the ventricular haul*: L.A., Rome, ReyKjaViK. London, Lagos, Sydney. Passports out; tickets ready—No Screaming; *Do Not Pull Your Fingernails Off*; Currency EXchange & Duty Free SaliVa: all aVailable once you have passed through security → just follow the lanEs and the siGns on the floor for diRECTions → make sure you have any elEctronic eQuipment out → and any liquids on display in one of the clear plastic bags provided → Do you have any liQuId? CleAr. PlAstic. BAgs. Ex-EX-EXcuse me, mam, do you have any liquid? Mam?

 Mam?

   Mam?

     Mam?

"Do you have any liquids inside your case?"

The young Thai woman working as the security screener stepped back a little, unsure what it was she was confronting. Her job (during this thirty-minute section of her shift) was to make sure customers navigated the roped lanes in an orderly fashion and removed any of the listed items for presentation at the x-ray machine. But the confused looking white woman in the immodest purple dress seemed to be having trouble with these tasks. Even before reaching the checkpoint she'd knocked over a stanchion and spent a number of minutes looking intently at the ceiling. Now that she'd tottered her way to the entrance of the bag check it was obvious something was wrong with her: she could hardly stand; she was wearing sunglasses inside; the muscles in her neck appeared to have given way and her head was flopping back and forth. "Mam," the scanner asked again in her professional English. "Do you have any liquids in your case?"

This time an answer arrived; the white woman seemed to have realised that she was being addressed. "Wata?" It nearly resembled a word, although it was followed by a less coherent emission, a half grunt, half moan: "Haauannng." The woman's jaw was locked and twisted, as if she were in a permanent state of trying to remove wedged food from a rear molar with her tongue. But rather than drag Sophie aside, the security scanner—who, despite working in customs, was young enough to have affinities for liberal flamboyance—merely ushered her politely to the bag check (*"This way, madam, if you please*") and indicated the conveyor belt that fed luggage into the x-ray machine. She even helped Sophie lift her carry-on up to the table, her arms seemingly too wobbly and ineffectual to manage on their own. Because there would be nothing worse than dragging this lady aside only to find out she was intellectually disabled. Wasn't it entirely possible for really attractive people to have special needs, or some exotic nerve and muscle condition, or to suffer from profound deafness and anxiety? And what was so wrong with a woman in her situation trying to look fashionable? The rock-star sunglasses, tousled hair, the chic strapless dress with passport and ticket tucked in at breast level—*how cool!* Although the heels really did seem like a safety hazard—because with whatever was going on with this chick, she was walking like a freshly birthed giraffe... So the scanner simply looked on as Sophie staggered to her left, then to her right, trying to line herself up for her approach to the metal detector. You *go* girl, she thought. And she felt no guilt about this, because if the woman actually was a drugged-out mess, then she had about sixty seconds left.

And then lots of things all happened at once.

At his desk behind the bulk of the x-ray machine, the on-duty operator pushed the freeze button so that he could more closely inspect the innards of Sophie's case. The contents came up on his screen as an array of shapes and colours, luminous and festive. First, the dark blue streak indicated what was metallic. From shape alone this appeared to be a large knife. Second, the highlighter green forms indicated what was less dense and most likely made of plastic. Here the shapes were more intricate but still obvious: a bundle of syringes at one end of the bag, a bulky artificial phallus at the other. Finally, there was the blob of glowing orange, smack (*yup*) bang in the centre. This, the scanner knew, indicated the existence of an organic compound. Based on the company it was keeping inside the case, it probably wasn't jam. "Shit," he said in Thai.

He waved over a colleague. The colleague gave a quick squint at the screen, covered his mouth with his hand, and then pushed the red button. The conveyor belt jerked to life again, and as Sophie's case rattled back out into the open the machine automatically siphoned it into a lane of its own. They watched as it bumped lazily down a series of rollers and came to a halt on the table reserved for inspection. Both men got up and moved toward it.

At exactly the same time, Sophie herself was trying to stand between the arches of the metal detector, but the gap for her passage was too small and she kept having to touch the sides to keep her balance, her lopsided weight threatening to knock the whole mechanism over—which was beeping frenetically anyway because she kept leaning back and forward and triggering the pulse induction, her earrings and her bangles and her rings and her sunglasses all setting it off. And in the commotion of it all the people behind her were starting to stare, and the security officers at the other detectors were losing focus, and the two x-ray operators who were at this very moment clutching

Sophie's carry-on were looking over and connecting the fracas with its owner—the lurching white woman in the purple dress. Everyone was watching. Watching as the security officer with the metal-detecting wand led her through and asked her to stand very still so he could swipe her down, but first could she please remove her sunglasses and her shoes. And though her head was lolling in spasticated circles she seemed to hear this request. Except first she had to pull down her dress, sending her passport and ticket to the floor and exposing both of her breasts, and it was then and only then that her hand managed to make it to her face to peel off her butterfly frames.

The security officer, despite being only a foot from her, was not the first to see it. Instinct meant he saw her areolae, then her dropped documents, then modesty kicked in and he turned his head away and held up his hand, trying to find the English words to get Sophie to cover herself. So it was left to a woman behind him who'd been collecting a laptop from the conveyer belt and happened to be looking back at the whole noisy fuss: she was the first to scream.

Then there was pointing. And gasping. And someone shouted, "Doctor!" in Thai—"This woman needs a fucking doctor!"

Sophie's eyeball had burst, its gelatinous structure deflating bizarrely inside its socket as blood began gushing tap-like down the left side of her face and onto her naked chest.

Yet this was only the most visible and therefore

incredible symptom of what was happening to her internally at that moment—the hideous confluence of narcotic explosions all peaking at once—and even before they could lay her on her back she was starting to seize, her whole body convulsing with violent spasms and cell-tearing tremors, bilious foam surging up and out of her mouth like a devilchild's baking-soda volcano, her mind boiling and fragmenting like overcooked fish meat. A drug dog suddenly began barking, awakened by its training. Then the crowd started pushing forward, hooking themselves up and around and trying to get a look at what was going on before the customs officers and security officials pulled themselves together and regained control of the situation—*Stand aside, please! Stand aside!*—shuffling gawkers away and ushering the public urgently toward the remaining checkpoints, cordoning off the semi-naked British woman as she lay haemorrhaging blood and existence and still trying to speak through the catastrophic throbbing: "*Step free, step free!*"

Howler monkeys screaming in the darkness of the branches.

Howler monkeys laughing.

Step 3.

What was Step 3?

What a spectacle, thought Quack. He sipped his takeaway coffee, watching from a safe distance as the mob at the security gate thronged around Sophie's ferocious and utterly resplendent distress. What a monstrous and fantastic spectacle! He was very nearly in awe. The girl was an abhorrent demon, a disgusting termagant in every respect. But there was no argument as to whether or not she'd done her job. She'd fulfilled her role superbly, captivating the audience with a display of total and unmitigated human horror—a macabre and perfectly timed main attraction. Now she was lying there with her nipples exposed and a hole for an eyeball, a phlegmy Western cynosure of sex and drugs and diversionary blood. And this is how she would die, her body gurgling on the floor of a foreign airport, what was left of her brain still trying to make it onto a flight she was never meant to get to. And all the while the *actual* mules were passing safely through the gates and boarding, families in fact, all non-descript and all smiling, all cheap but highly reliable labour in their own right—each member of the workforce transporting their own internalised and well-wrapped package that, unlike Sophie's, would neither open nor decay until it reached its destination.

Job done, Quack thought. He was overcome with a sense of professional satisfaction. He finished his coffee and turned to go.

INT. RESORT FRONT DESK – MORNING

Mike Murphy was waiting at the front desk while outside his two boys played on the family's stack of luggage and Eleanor stood sucking on a cigarette, squashing its filter between her thumb and index finger with an addict's intensity. He was becoming concerned. At first he'd thought maybe his wife was simply being kooky by claiming some cosmic bad feeling and feigning the sudden urge to fumigate herself—she was that kind of interesting and beautifully capricious woman. But this was turning into more than a passing eccentricity. Hopefully, he thought, it was just something to do with the place, some Thai thing, like an abstract parasite she would shed once she was safely on the plane back to Chicago. With any luck customs would catch and kill whatever bad juju she was carting around before they even took off. Not that he believed in anything like that, but, you know…

He turned back to the desk and hit the service bell again, its chime lingering like a balloon in the cavern of the reception area, and within a moment the concierge appeared, an intelligent-looking young man with a responsible haircut and a thick Australian accent that connected in Mike's memory immediately. "Sorry to keep you waiting, sir. How can I help?"

"Just checking out and handing back the keys."

"Of course, sir. You must be the Murphys." His manner was effusive as he reached out to take the room key. "And how was your stay with us?"

"It was you, wasn't it?"

The concierge paused in his movement. His smile was thoroughly disarming: "Sorry, sir, but I have a policy of not answering questions if they have the potential to incriminate me."

"It's a good policy," Mike laughed. "Pleading the Fifth. No, I called the desk a few nights ago when the sultry but…" he searched for the word, "*dense* British couple had their screaming match. It must have been you who comped us. Unless there's another Aussie working here.'

"Just me, sir."

"Well, thankyou—that was beyond decent and I don't think we deserved it."

"Of course you did. Please understand, sir, that…" He glanced over Mike's shoulder in a quick but controlled fashion, checking, it seemed, that they were definitely alone. "Can I speak to you in confidence for a moment?"

"Sure. By which you mean *don't repeat this*, right? Like, not on a travel website…?"

The concierge gave the tiniest of affirmatory nods. "You were here to have a good time away from whatever travails and routines befall you in regular life. I understand that completely. And this place is far too exorbitant for you and your family to have to concern yourselves with even the slightest inconvenience. The fact you alerted me to the disturbance at all was supremely human and something I appreciated greatly. Comping the rest of your stay was the least I could do."

This short speech washed over Mike. It was eloquent, it acknowledged him, it made him feel important. It made him respect the younger man immediately without losing any face. "You're gonna go a long way in this business," he said, his tone more avuncular than he would have liked. "Is this what you do, here? Is this your fulltime thing, I mean? You just seem like you should be doing more than looking after the likes of me. And I mean no offence by that."

The concierge laughed. "Not at all, sir. It's a pleasure."

"But seriously…"

The Australian took a second and rested his hands on the edge of the desk, taking the weight of his body on his forearms. "This lifestyle suits me," he said contemplatively. "There's actually lots of varied freelance work, and the hours are flexible. For example, I'm off all next week."

"What are you going to do with the time?"

Again, he considered his answer. "Sir, are you *sure* you want to know about the mundane minutiae of my life? It's customary for the *concierge* to ask these questions of the departing guest, not the other way around. That's the convention of this context."

"Please," Mike insisted. "I'm *un*conventional. Shoot."

"Okay." He smiled. "Well, there's an island out there." He pointed out the side doors at the beach chalets and the sea beyond. "It's about five kilometres—three-ish miles to an American. Anyway, it's cut off—no digital amenities or anything, no law. Everyone on it is pretty much a Western refugee to psychedelia: mushrooms, LSD, all manner of chemically-customised exotica that reorganizes the grey matter in ways that are, well, Frankensteinian. So I'm taking a little boat and heading out there."

"To join in!?"

"Oh, no. I'm much too responsible. But these guys make *ideal* candidates for one of the other industries I'm connected with. I source—what's the best way to put this?—*free-range* meat for a bourgeoning market of executive cannibals. It's good work, the setting's nice, and frankly I feel like I'm giving back. Most of the space heads out there have served their useful purpose, so it's good to see them flourish in a new role."

Mike was grinning. "I'm sure the money for work like

that is nothing to sneeze at. Probably requires a whole set of niche skills, too."

"Absolutely. But it's never about the money. Challenge, diversity, that's what creates job fulfilment."

"Too true."

Outside, Eleanor was lighting a fresh cigarette while still in the process of stubbing out the last, and even as she was inhaling the hot nicotine from her new smoke she was thinking about how much she would enjoy the next one. Jason and Matthew were stacking and unstacking the family's bags, an activity she'd decided was extremely irritating, however she was too preoccupied with smoking to do anything about it. On top of it all there was the constant humming dread—the cold sense that terrible things were happening, or had happened, would happen again—and she'd decided that it was the place, this resort, this sunlight, maybe all of Thailand, and she wanted nothing more than to be away from it.

The airport shuttle arrived at the same time the automatic glass doors slid open and her husband came strolling out, his gently balding pate growing ever nearer to glinting, his stomach beginning to cling to even his loosest shirts. "Nice guy," he said as he crossed the pavement to the driveway, a smile on his face.

"What? Who?"

"Concierge. Guy that comped us."

"Oh."

As the shuttle driver descended to help Mike stow the

family's luggage, the twins climbed aboard. She was starting to feel ill, perspiration beading at her temples and her stomach bubbling and heaving like hot stew in a rocking cauldron. "Did you ask him what happened with the couple?"

"What? No, of course not. None of my business—nor yours, you prurient wench. Now *please* put that death stick out so we can go." Mike turned and started to board the shuttle.

Eleanor looked back toward the reception desk, but the doors had already closed and all she could see beyond her own reflection was the vaguest of human outlines.

INT. EXECUTIVE OFFICE – LATE AFTERNOON

"…the airport shuttle pulls away and the camera pans to follow it. The sound of the engine recedes and we can hear the almost imperceptible emergence of a disquieting non-diegetic hum, one that fizzes electrically, like it's coming from high-tension powerlines. The camera continues its smooth pan and dollys forward into a wide-shot of the automatic doors, which open to reveal Jack as he walks out into the light, the lens moving closer and closer in its unsettling push until we have a close-up that mirrors the very first shot of the film." The filmmaker pauses and looks at the exec to ensure he understands the genius of this symmetrical imagery. "It's Jack's face, staring in a tight and almost Kubrickian fashion past the lens, the lethal trilling of the soundtrack rising to its boil-point crescendo. We *get* the evil behind this look now. The amorality. The tiger. We know it. Then BANG! Cut to black screen and we're out!"

Rain is pelting the windows and the sky has darkened considerably.

Before saying anything, the exec stands and moves to the lamp in the corner of the room and switches it on. The light it provides is weak, but the warm peach glow helps to offset the growing drear. He crouches down next to Henry the bullmastiff and rubs his coat affectionately. The dog lets out a drowsy and restrained bark of assent, then the exec sits back in his swivel chair and examines the glass of teenage blood, reaching out and moving it a fraction to the left, disturbing the content only slightly. "Benny really should have provided a coaster for this," he says. "Guess he fell down on that one."

The filmmaker remains waiting, reluctant to say any more before the exec does. He is confident that between his verbal skill and the sophistication of his narrative he has wowed the exec, and that this reserve on the exec's part is simply part of the game the two of them must now play.

"Okay, Max…" The exec lingers. "You want to know what I'm thinking…?"

"That's why I'm here, right? That's the point of the pitch. I'm pitching to *you*."

The exec drags the tip of his index finger across the varnished desktop as if he's trying to collect dust, although there is no dust there. To the filmmaker, it seems like the exec's finger is being pursued by a line of rapidly vanishing condensation.

"Okay." The exec puts both palms flat on the desk, shifts himself into it, and sits up very straight so his bellybutton is roughly the height of its edge. He breathes in deeply and slowly, looking a little to his left at some non-specific point in the room. He turns to the filmmaker. "Are you prepared for this, Max?"

"Sure."

"Because there's some good stuff in there. The destructive power of Olly's organs once they've left his body: great. It's even almost a happy ending of sorts. Sophie's foaming death-twist at the airport: fantastic—it needed that. It doesn't even matter that there's probably no combination of drugs anywhere that can make an eyeball pop. But so what, right? The whole film takes liberties with its creative license and it's better for it. The events in the final act will also compel a certain type of viewer to go right back to the start and watch it again to see if they can pick up all the little hints and cues."

"Thanks."

"But let's start with something relatively small." The exec drums a short beat with his fingers on the wood. "The Murphys—they take up quite a bit of the middle section, and I've gotta say, I don't really understand the smoking. Why has Eleanor suddenly picked up the habit?"

"Look, I've explained the existence of the Murphys already. They're in it to balance out the personalities in the central story. They're the *control* in the experiment. They help the audience gauge Olly's irrationality and measure Jack's evil in a clear fashion, rather than forcing them to pick a side because they have nothing to compare them against."

"They could compare them against themselves?"

"No they can't, and certainly not during the turmoil of actually watching it a first time round. The Murphys *need* to be there. And the smoking… Really, you don't get the smoking?"

"It just seems like it's badly thought out," says the exec. His face is blank and unemotional. "It seems like the whole family's been thrust into the centre of the narrative without any propulsive significance and so you've found a weak way to keep them connected until the end, when in actual fact they're totally superfluous."

"No! Shit no! They're indispensable!" The filmmaker jerks forward. He becomes loud and aggressive in a way he has not yet been. "No, the sudden existence of this intersubjective psychological link between Eleanor and the Olly/Jack interaction is meant to signal the possibility of there being more to life and existence than we can see. God, the Devil, alternate dimensions! Something great. And because Eleanor's inexplicably psychically linked to something toxic, she ends up being sort of possessed to smoke—it's like a tiny appeal to evil and the supernatural. And that's meant to jar against the atheistic, existential, empirical approach of Jack. The two forces are meant to be floating together in the background of the narrative. Binary oppositions. Something versus nothing. It's *intentional*. It's designed to foster a philosophical tension."

The exec looks at the filmmaker carefully. "Okay. I'm

willing to overlook the pretention and buy that, but I don't think others will. Because that's really the next big problem with this, Max. Who are we seriously going to market this to? What's the demographic this is aiming at? What's your genre?"

The filmmaker answers without even pausing: "It's an erotic and surrealistic body horror thriller with elements of black comedy and an art house sensibility."

"Fuck off, Max. What's it actually *about?*"

"Look, frankly, don't you think it's nice if the audience works that out for themselves. Isn't that, you know, kind of the very personal point of art, to engage with it *individually*."

"Don't dodge this."

"I'm not. It's just not about one straightforward thing, is all. You know, it's not about one easy thematic thing. It's about lots of things."

"Like?"

"Okay. It's about the perils of trust. It's about personal autonomy, human entanglements, and definitions of masculinity. It's about madness and relationships and the obvious disconnection between us all in a globalized society. It's about the destructive power of love and our capacity to be so irrational it destroys us. And it's about human worth: about our objective value in a world that tells us we have some, but then doesn't follow through in the fabric of our real lives."

The exec stares inscrutably at the filmmaker, who clearly believes his answer is a good one. "That's amazingly pretentious, Max. That's an incredible level of fluff. Tell me what the film's actually about in two sentences. What happens? Not themes. I want the story for the back of the DVD cover."

This stumps the filmmaker. He chews the knuckle on his index finger as he thinks. "When an attractive working class couple take their dream holiday in Thailand, things get out of hand after they…" His knuckle goes back between his teeth and his brow compresses like an accordion.

"Try again."

"When Olly's relationship ends while on holiday, he finds himself caught in an increasingly menacing web of… Fuck!"

"Admit it. You're pitching a schlock film about internet porn, drug mules and comical organ trading. It's niche. It has a *tiny* audience. There's no sense in pretending this film can be marketed as anything other than that, especially with all the dick and blood. And I'm personally in favour of those things—they're entertaining—but you have to know what it is you're peddling. You can't pour people gasoline and say it's champagne."

"Hey, you know we do that all the time in this industry. But you're wrong. The art, it's in the direction. It's in the casting and cinematography. It's not the content."

"Max, there are problems right in the heart of this thing that mean it's never going to resonate with a wide audience no matter who directs or who stars. One problem would be fine, but there are too many here. First off, it's mean. It's a horrendously and relentlessly mean film where terrible things happen to virtually everyone, and no one of significance is likeable unless you're an angry teen sociopath who fantasizes about power and control."

"But–"

"On top of that, the story structure is floppy. The mid-section is weak and slow moving, needlessly obtuse in its choice of perspectives–"

"I disagree!–"

"–and there's no genuine protagonist. Olly's an uninspiring failure. And you can't argue Jack's an anti-hero, because he's not characterised enough to claim that kind of centrality. He's not really even an anti-hero in nature, he's just selfish, coldly destructive and remorseless. I also noticed the thing doesn't pass the Bechdel—which isn't a prerequisite in and of itself, but in this case the narrative is built around some quite misogynistic themes. It could have been penned by an incel."

"A what?"

"An involuntary celibate. A hate-filled neckbeard. A male so angry at women because they won't have sex with him that he creates shit like this where woman are treated with the same delicacy as blacks were in *Birth of a Nation*. It's a kind of propaganda."

"Come on! What about Elea–"

"I'm not finished. It's also racist. I shouldn't even

have to tell you why. And it's tonally inconsistent."

"You've said that already."

"And it *has no point*. That's one of the big things, something that lodges like a bullet in my gut. There is absolutely no reason this should exist as a film."

The filmmaker has become manic in his defence: "Yeah, but, doesn't that apply to everything?"

"Everything! That's another great point!" the exec exclaims. This is the first time he has truly raised his voice. "Let's add that to the pile too! Because who the fuck are *we*?" He spreads his hands to encompass the office.

"What do you mean?"

"You and me! You know exactly what I mean, Max. *Exactly* what I mean."

The filmmaker gets up from his chair and walks over toward the wall. He is clearly dejected. His face has drained of the enthusiasm and energy that defined it during his pitch. "So it's a no go, then?" he asks, although it's barely a question.

The exec rolls away from his desk and spins his chair to look out the rainy window. "I didn't say that." He looks across the sodden murk of the city, then spins his chair back to his desk. "In fact, I am prepared to green-light this picture. I'm prepared to have this become a reality—one in which I'll not only push this through to production but make sure you have total creative control. No fiddling. No rewrites. No studio fuck-arounds."

The filmmaker turns slowly and sceptically. "*Really*? You just savaged it. And you're right, too. That's the worst part—about a lot of it, you're right." He looks back at the wall.

The exec points to the bullmastiff but does not look at it. "Why do you think I have the dog here, Max? Why do you think I had Benny go out and purchase big old Henry here?"

The filmmaker rotates again. He is despondent. With his back to the wall he slides down it until he is sitting on the floor, his knees pointing at the ceiling and his hands on the carpet. Because he is an adult male in an office setting, the posture makes him look ludicrous. "Honestly… based on earlier discussion, I presumed you were going to involve it in some sex thing with your wife—or a hooker, I don't know, just, you know…" He shrugs his shoulders.

"And how about the blood here, Max? What do you think the point of that was?"

The filmmaker stares vaguely over at the glass. "Meh. I don't know. I figured you were making a gaudy point about your own capacity for senseless excess. Or about your power… Seemed funny at the time."

The exec is unfazed, his features passive. "Do you know nothing about story structure?" The exec stretches his arms to their full wingspan to illustrate everything: his question, his disappointment, his desire to keep the filmmaker listening. "Clearly not as much as you should or as much as you think you do." His palms drop back down on the desk as he becomes emphatic. "Now I'm absolutely serious about what I'm going to say next. Are you listening?"

"Yeah. Yeah, I'm listening."

The exec stands up and moves to the right front edge of his desk. He is looking down at the filmmaker, who is still sitting against the wall. "Nothing I'm about to say is a joke or a metaphor or has a hidden meaning. It's all very literal. All very straightforward. Do you understand?"

"Yes. You're about to say something serious. I get it."

"Because I *will* let you make your film if you do the following…"

The filmmaker looks up. "Do what?"

The exec steps forward and squats down on his haunches. Even from this lowered position he is still taller than the slumped filmmaker. It looks like he might be preparing to pounce. "It seems to me (and correct me if I'm wrong) that you think it's absolutely fine to inflict suffering on your characters—to hurt them. That it's completely okay."

"Of course. They're fictional."

"Nothing is fictional, Max—especially not characters. And you want yours to exist in tortured perpetuity."

"What? Look–"

"If you want to spawn a reality of such horror and misery, and then subject your characters to the purgatory of it forever and ever, then you must make a proper offering. You, of all people, should realise the power and significance of creation—and especially in this case, given the pain you will be bringing into the world. You, in your own way, must make a sacrifice for them. You need to prove they are worthy of sincere creation by genuflecting to higher concepts; you need to prove that you are worthy yourself."

"Sacrifice? What the hell are you talking about? They're *fictional* characters! You can pull their eyeballs out and have them fuck their mothers and it doesn't matter."

"Yes. It does. I'm not joking, Max." The steel blankness of the exec's voice holds the filmmaker in place. "I know you want this film made. But you have to demonstrate the ferocity of your commitment to it. I *will* green-light this film. Right now. Guaranteed. And you can do whatever you want with it. Solid sixty-million budget. Total creative control. I just want two things."

The filmmaker's face seems to smooth out and he starts to sit up. "Sixty-million?"

"For just two things."

"…What?"

"Two clearly defined things, and you can have it all."

"What? Jesus!" The filmmaker scrambles up so he too is on his haunches, squatting forwards and staring into the eyes of the exec. The two men look like they are about to sumo wrestle.

"Drink the blood, then kill the dog."

"Fuck off!" The filmmaker stands quickly and moves to the window, highly offended. "You're a massive asshole. You know that?"

"Drink the blood, then kill the dog." The exec stands as well, although his movement has the steadiness and equilibrium of certainty. "Do that right now, and you can make this film."

"You're serious…?"

"You have sixty seconds to start."

"Huh?"

"Sixty seconds to start. Then you can have your film. I don't mind how long it takes to kill Henry—that's not a factor, provided there's a sustained commitment to the task—but you have sixty seconds to start. Fifty-nine. Fifty-eight. Fifty-seven–"

"You know this is insane, right?"

"Fifty-four. Fifty-three–"

"Why are you fucking with me? Is someone filming this? Is this a reality show thing or something?"

"Forty-eight. No, Max. It's not being filmed. This is a real situation and a real offer. Forty-four. Forty-three. Forty-two."

"It's crazy."

"Forty."

"How do I know you'll even go through with it? How do I know you won't just, you know, have me blacklisted?"

"Thirty-five. You have my word. Thirty-three."

"Your word?"

The exec is nodding and looking at the filmmaker as he counts, and the filmmaker knows now, with all the force of a natural disaster, that the exec is telling him the truth. "Twenty-four. Twenty-three. Twenty-two—"

As the exec continues counting, the filmmaker turns unsteadily, like he is looking for something. His breathing has become desperate and uneven, although he has already made his choice. There's really no question. He moves suddenly and with resolution to the desk and picks up the glass of blood. He is determined to have it all go down in one. He puts it to his lips, spilling some of it on his fingers and his jacket in the process, and starts to glug it back.

"Atta-boy!" the exec yells. He stops counting, but his energy and enthusiasm for what is taking place creates an even greater atmosphere of urgency in the room. The filmmaker works fast, slurping, his pupils constricted to tiny pinpricks, his body rigid in the process of ingestion. "Get it all down! Do it, Max! Chug that virgin's plasma!"

The filmmaker finishes the blood, runnels of it vampirically sluicing across his chin. He looks at the exec and then hurls the empty glass against the wall where it shatters into a pinkly spattered blast-pattern. The violence of it all startles the bullmastiff and it clambers to its paws and barks apprehensively.

"Now the dog!" the exec yells. "*Et potestas tenebrarum.* Do it now, before your purpose cools!"

The filmmaker lunges toward the canine, grabbing it by its thickened neck with both hands, trying to find a way to dig in. But the dog is big and muscular. Its shoulders are strong, and it starts to fight, wriggling and barking to get free, its paws looking for purchase against the filmmaker's trousers as the he tries frantically to pick it up, his arms shifting around the animal's neck. "*Aperire portas!*" the exec bellows. His voice is triumphant, but neither Henry nor the filmmaker pay him any attention. The filmmaker is determined to twist the dog's head as violently as he can, to snap its spinal cord, but the animal is writhing, snarling, its teeth hunting for any kind of meat and its blackened muzzle jutting into the air, and in this frenzy it is hard for the filmmaker to get the firm grip he needs. He tries to hook the dog around its back and thread his arm up through its front legs (*if he can get a hold of its collar then he can try to gouge its eyes out*) but the dog slips free and turns and bites him hard, taking vice-like hold of the filmmaker's forearm. He screams in pain, but he is by no means done. With the bullmastiff's jaw clamped on his arm and its weight pressing down on him, the filmmaker starts punching the dog in the head, screaming and punching, the dog growling, and then he goes for the softness of the dog's left eye with his thumb. "*Concurrere virgo est sanguis!*" In the commotion of it all he doesn't register the rising voice of the exec, the initial dirge of recitation behind the chaos escalating into the deep and protracted cry of a man seeking another world: "*Stulti et indignatio!*" The bullmastiff is threshing like a shark on the deck of a boat and the filmmaker is trying to wrestle its back onto the carpet and pin it down—"*Victimam grandem super animali!*"—his own flesh torn but now free of the dog's teeth, his face contorted into the mangled asymmetry of a starving fiend. "*Flores in ugbay!*" The eyes of the exec are wide open, hungry, locked on the tangle of suffering on the office floor. Rain continues to pelt the windows. "*Culus! Culus! Culus!*" The dog is howling now. It knows it won't be long.

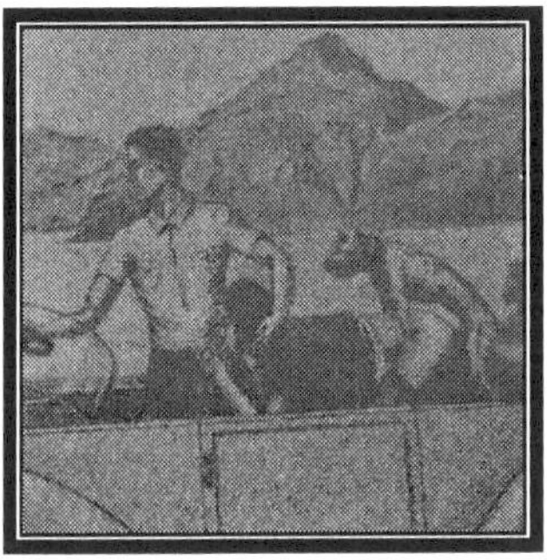

ABOUT THE AUTHOR

Josh Caverton is from West Auckland, New Zealand.

Printed in Great Britain
by Amazon